HEART OF ICE

Jean Morrant

CHIVERS

British Library Cataloguing in Publication Data available

This Large Print edition published by BBC Audiobooks Ltd, Bath, 2009.
Published by arrangement with the author.

U.K. Hardcover ISBN 978 1 408 43278 5
U.K. Softcover ISBN 978 1 408 43279 2

LP

Printed and bound in Great Britain by
CPI Antony Rowe, Chippenham and Eastbourne

CHAPTER ONE

'That's all I need . . .' Kate muttered to herself as a flurry of snowflakes swept across the windscreen of her car. And as the sign 'To the North' loomed at the roadside, she sighed and straightened her aching shoulders, considering again the reason for her journey.

'Katherine?' her father had begun when she'd picked up the telephone the previous evening, and she had known immediately he had some request to make which may not meet with her approval. He always used her full name when about to cajole her and she had been instantly on her guard.

'A trip up north will do you good,' he'd insisted when she protested at his suggestion, and went on to say, 'I've had a word with the physiotherapist. He expects you to be leading a fairly normal life by now, providing you have persevered with the exercises, which means you can soon resume playing the piano. Meanwhile, you must keep that arm moving—keep the muscles in trim.'

And before she had the opportunity to further her protest, he'd added quickly, 'As Godfrey will be busy during the next few weeks booking artistes for this forthcoming show, there's nothing to keep you in London, is there? In any case no-one could persuade your old nanny to go into a nursing home—she insisted upon returning to the cottage—you know what Martha's like. Even so, I'm rather concerned about her being up there alone, and rather vulnerable, I fear.'

Kate had asked if anyone else would be calling on her—a nurse maybe . . . But her father had cut in to assure her that medical attention would be available, of course, also visits from the district nurse. Then he had paused a moment before continuing impatiently, 'Well, come on, darling, you once did a spell of work in a hospital ward so what do you say?'

It had been a poor line from Rome and any further details were not too clear when his voice kept fading. However, she had finally agreed to his appeal; it was hopeless to even attempt to refuse her father anything. There again, he was right about the exercise; after she'd broken her wrist—a rather complicated fracture—and returned from hospital she had needed treatment for a considerable length of time. There had been so little to do in her flat, and Godfrey had been too occupied with his agency work to give her much of his time. Come to think of it, she hadn't seen Godfrey Downes for almost three weeks, and that had been only a brief visit. But he still insisted, once she was able, he would get her a lengthy booking with a well-known orchestra.

Even though the physiotherapist had passed

her fit to play the piano almost a month ago, Godfrey didn't want her to rush things, said he was worried a too early return to playing would do her wrist harm. But now she was beginning to doubt him; maybe it would be wiser not to be so easily available when next he chose to call. Her father had made such a remark more than once and perhaps it was sound advice.

Up on the wild Yorkshire moors, cut off from all that was familiar—and the telephone in the cottage out of order—would give her an opportunity to reconsider her future. If Godfrey was to continue to act as her agent, then it was time he had something more positive to offer. She loved her music, it was true but, until the accident, her earnings from the piano recitals in little known venues hardly covered her living expenses and she didn't want to depend upon her father to supplement her earnings.

But her father had assured her he was content to provide for her and repeated again how much she would love the tranquillity of the place. 'A new telephone line will be installed, but until it is connected use your mobile so that I can give you an occasional call. But don't allow anyone into the cottage,' he had advised, 'unless they are known to Martha, of course.'

'It all sounds very mysterious.' She'd laughed. 'Are you anticipating trouble?'

'No, but I've asked a friend of mine to keep an eye on things, just in case there's anything you're worried about.'

Kate had smiled to herself. It was almost five years since she had seen the retired housekeeper who had cared for her after her mother died. She recalled Martha's cheerful disposition, and was thankful her speech had been only slightly affected when she suffered her stroke.

Kate's progress through the historic city of York was slow. The traffic-filled streets were thronged with bargain hunters in the early January sales, and by the time she reached the small market town of Elmsgarth, some twenty-five miles farther north, darkness was beginning to descend.

Turning off the main road, she changed down a gear, preparing to take the approaching hill, relieved to see a man with a large shovel spreading grit over the surface. Huge snowflakes were falling on the windscreen, clogging the wipers until she had to stop and clear them before she could continue along the narrowing road when she felt the occasional slide of the rear wheels as she travelled over the uneven surface.

It grew even darker as a pine wood closed in at the roadside and the car slid drunkenly across the ungritted surface when she braked at an approaching ford. Thankfully, it was dry and aided by the shelter from the trees she was able to negotiate the steep rise on the other side without too much difficulty.

'Oh, no!' she muttered to herself, alighting from the vehicle yet again to clear the wipers of hard-packed snow. What had possessed her to agree to this crazy journey when she could have been tucked away in her cosy little flat with Godfrey for company? But she had to remind herself, Godfrey hadn't been near for some time.

With icy flakes of snow swirling into every gap in her clothing, once the wipers were successfully cleared she was thankful to get back inside. Blowing warm breath into her cupped hands, she wondered exactly how much further she must drive in these conditions. But this time when she tried to pull away, the car refused to move. Instead, she uttered a fresh sigh of exasperation over the whine of spinning tyres.

In the driving seat she began to shiver and a sob of frustration tinged with despair caught in her throat. There was only one course left to her, she would have to abandon the car and walk. But how far must she go in these conditions before she reached the cottage? She felt isolated and increasingly afraid, and when suddenly a hand cleared a patch on the outside of the windscreen and a face appeared in its place, she uttered a startled cry and went rigid in her seat.

'What the devil are you doing here?' a male

voice thundered as the door beside her was wrenched open. 'You'll freeze to death!'

Her feeling of terror was quickly replaced by one of relief, yet his disparaging tone annoyed her.

'I would have thought it obvious,' she replied coolly. 'My car's stuck fast.'

The tweed-hatted newcomer regarded her sternly through the open door, his eyes narrowing. 'It's obvious you're a stranger to these parts,' he countered, 'or you wouldn't have attempted the journey on a night such as this.'

'And you don't sound like a local, so how come you're here?' she challenged, noting his slight Scottish accent.

Ignoring her question he asked, 'Where are you heading?'

'Hawthorn Cottage. Is it far from here?'

'Little more than a mile, but it's a treacherous road.' He gave a slight shake of his head. 'What ever possessed you to drive in these conditions?'

'How was I to know what the weather conditions would be!' she exclaimed crossly. 'As it happens I had no choice, the lady at Hawthorn expects me. She's been ill, you see, needs someone to care for her.'

'You mean Miss Cussons?' he asked slowly, then gave a knowing nod.

'That's right.'

'At least that is something to your credit,' he

countered. 'Now, hand me the keys to the boot and we'll see what can be done. You are carrying a shovel?'

'Shovel?' she echoed. 'Well, no, I wouldn't have thought it would be necessary . . .'

'Just as I expected!' He gave an impatient click of his tongue. 'Obviously, you're used to city life . . .'

'And what if I am!' she bristled. 'At least we're more civilised! I suppose I should have expected something like this in such a place.'

'Whatever you may think of your location, there's no point in sitting there arguing,' he said briskly. 'Let's see what we can find to put under the wheels and get you out of this mess—perhaps the car mats will do the trick.'

'Car mats . . . ?'

'Yes, don't just sit there, girl!'

Hating his autocratic manner, she merely shot him an icy stare, knowing she was in no position to argue.

'If we don't do something very soon you'll never get away!' he said sharply. 'Unless you prefer to stay here all night?'

Biting back a sharp retort, she stepped out into the deepening snow and, as he straightened, in the light from the car's interior, she saw he was quite tall and suitably dressed for the weather in high, polished boots and a heavy weatherproof coat.

Reaching into the car, he took out the protective rubber mats and went to slide them under the rear wheels. And slipping back into the driving seat he started the engine, but still the car refused to pull away. There was the spinning of rubber followed by muffled curses before he got out to remonstrate with her further.

'You've allowed the wheels to spin far too long—it's a sheet of ice under there—trust a woman to do a stupid thing like that!'

Bristling with indignation, she spun round on him and cried furiously, 'If all you can do is criticise, then please go, I'll manage on my own!'

Straightening, he towered above her, his dark eyes glinting in the dim glow of light. 'Right now, I don't like being here anymore than you do!' he hissed, 'but neither do I care for the idea of leaving anyone to freeze to death—even you!'

Having the alternative put to her so bluntly, she became more subdued, and clutching her coat tightly around her chilled body, she stifled her indignation.

'I'm sorry,' she began, 'by the way, where's your vehicle?'

'Over there,' he said, his expression softening a little, and nodded towards the nearby clump of trees as he made a soft clicking noise with his tongue. Suddenly there was movement close by, accompanied by the sound of heavy breathing, causing Kate to gasp in alarm as she took a slithering step back.

Quickly extending his arm, he caught her before she lost her balance. 'Not frightened of horses, are you?' he asked with a short laugh as a massive chestnut hunter loomed into view.

'Oh no, I'm not frightened,' she breathed in relief, extricating herself from his hold. 'I just hadn't thought of you being on horseback.'

'It's the most reliable means of travel in this weather,' he said in a more even voice, 'and we don't usually experience the trouble you're having. Now, stay here whilst I fetch an armful of bracken—it may just solve our problem.'

Leaving her by the car he walked back towards the trees, returning moments later with a bundle of almost dry golden brown bracken which he placed in front of the rear wheels.

'In the shelter of the trees this keeps fairly dry so hopefully the tyres will get a grip,' he told her. 'Now, can you start the engine and move off very slowly when I tell you. If I push at the same time you should get away.'

Thanking him, she got in and put the car into gear, letting in the clutch as he had instructed. After a brief squeal of rubber the car moved forward onto level ground.

'You'll find it hard going,' he warned her through the open window, 'but I'll stay with you until you reach the cottage. Don't open the door to anyone unknown to you. I'll call in at Hawthorn and see how you're managing.'

'Thanks very much, I'm really grateful,' she

called, her spirits lifting now, 'but there's no need for you to call, as I understand someone will be keeping an eye on me whilst I'm here.'

'And who may that be?' he queried, stooping to look into the interior.

She laughed. 'I've no idea—my father didn't mention his name but I believe he lives at a place called Ivy Lodge. Probably a shooting friend of his. Some gout-ridden old squire smelling of animals . . .' She broke off and bit her lip. 'Sorry, I expect you're a farmer—didn't mean to be rude.'

'Well, he's got quite a task ahead of him, poor chap,' he remarked in severe tones, yet Kate was sure she saw the corners of his firm mouth twitch with what she took to be amusement.

Kate eased the car slowly forward, going ahead of him in the direction he'd indicated, hearing him call, 'Take care now, don't do anything silly, and keep your door locked . . .' as she passed.

'Arrogant beast!' she muttered to herself, though had to admit she would never have got on her way if it hadn't been for his assistance.

* * *

That night Kate slept soundly and it was already daylight when she rose from her warm bed to look through the window. The scene before her was breathtaking, causing her to gasp in surprise. Snow had drifted high against the wall of the house, sparkling white, and deeper than she would ever have thought possible.

She felt surprisingly well rested, and the problems connected with Godfrey and her future were miles away and she experienced a curious feeling of release, of freedom from emotional strain.

Since leaving London she'd had time to think, time to consider Godfrey in the role of her husband and ask herself if she loved him sufficiently to embark upon marriage. She uttered a deep, wavering sigh; was her father right? Was Godfrey the unsuitable match he considered him to be?

Deep in thought, she wandered into the newly installed, heated bathroom, which had been converted from the tiny box room previously used for storage. She regarded her reflection thoughtfully; her fair skin was smooth and her blue eyes bright after the sound sleep. Martha had been quite firm the night before, insisting they save the lengthier chats until she was well rested.

Donning a warm, fluffy housecoat, she went downstairs to put the kettle on for morning tea. It was curiously dark in the kitchen, and for a moment she thought she had left the curtains closed overnight. Then she realised snow had drifted over the window, almost blocking out the light.

Remembering Martha mentioning the light bulb had blown, she felt her way across the kitchen where she managed to light an oil lamp and thought the resulting effect, though unfamiliar to her, was extremely cosy.

Turning to the old black fireplace she saw, as Martha had told her, the district nurse had laid sticks and paper ready for lighting, and she soon had a good fire roaring up the chimney. But, barely fifteen minutes later, she was about to pour boiling water into the brown teapot, when she heard strange noises coming from somewhere outside. There was a curious scraping sound followed by a thud, and as it continued it seemed to come closer to the house.

As it was impossible to see anything through the snow-covered window she went to unlatch the door, quite unprepared for the wall of snow that fell inwards as she drew it back. The furry mules she wore offered little protection, and her first reaction when she felt the icy mass on her almost bare feet was to give a shriek of alarm. But the hoot of laughter that reached her from outside soon warmed her cheeks when she recognised it came from the man who had helped her the previous night.

'If all you can do is laugh . . .' she began then, overcome by annoyance, she tried to slam the door closed but the fall of snow prevented it.

There came another throaty chuckle and a

stamping of feet before the door opened once more and he stepped inside. He was carrying a shovel, which he used to scoop up the offending snow to return it to the garden.

'Glad you're not out in this, heh?' he asked smilingly. 'I've cleared a path for you to the fuel store.'

'Thank you, that was thoughtful of you.'

Standing with feet apart and back to the fire, he glanced over to the table. 'Brewing tea, are you? Good, a hot drink will be most welcome. It's quite sharp out there. If you like, I'll take one up for Martha.' He smiled as he added, 'That is, when you've stopped gaping at me as if I'd arrived from another planet.'

For a moment she was speechless then, finding her voice said sharply, 'I realise you've come to my aid twice already, for which I'm grateful. But I'm not used to strangers walking in like this, particularly as you were the one to warn me against it. Also, I'm not yet dressed,' she added defensively, glancing down at her thick, blue dressing gown.

'Not dressed?' he queried with a slightly wicked smile. 'I would say you are extremely well covered, and very prettily, too.'

Kate felt her colour rise and, to hide her embarrassment, concentrated on setting out cups and saucers. She considered his manner over-familiar, yet there was something disturbingly normal about his presence in the kitchen that made it difficult for her to ask him to leave.

'I'll take Martha her tea,' she said as she prepared a tray. 'She's in bed, you know.'

'I do know, and that's why I'm here,' he said with a grin. 'I'm quite used to seeing her in bed, Miss Prim, I'm her doctor.'

Kate's lips parted in surprise. 'Oh, I didn't know,' she managed at last. 'Now I realise why you came uninvited.'

'Protecting Martha's reputation, heh?' he said good-humouredly. 'Actually, I'm pleased you're here as I was becoming quite concerned about her being alone.'

'Yes, my father was worried about her, too. You see, for years she was our housekeeper and helped with my upbringing, so when she retired he suggested she make her home here as he only uses the place occasionally. She always wanted to return to the area where she grew up.'

He nodded. 'So I believe. Obviously, your father valued her service and I can well understand why. Although she has a heart of gold, Martha is nobody's fool, and I do believe some of her spirit has rubbed off on you.'

Seeing amusement in his twinkling, dark eyes she suppressed a sharp retort. 'I'll take that as a compliment,' she said lightly, and with a lift of her head, added, 'Martha taught me a great deal but she always gave me to understand it never pays to believe everything I'm told.'

'In London, maybe,' he countered with a quizzical gaze, 'but I think you'll find folk around here more sincere, and . . .'

'And outspoken,' she broke in crisply. 'In fact, one might say downright rude!'

He shot her a frowning glance. 'Well, Miss Wilson, are you going to stand there arguing for the rest of the morning, or do I get that cup of tea?'

Shooting him an icy look, Kate placed a cup and saucer before him and poured tea. 'Sugar perhaps?' she asked and slid the bowl towards him.

'No, thanks, but I'll take a lump for my mount. He deserves a treat this morning.'

'Do you always do your rounds on horseback?'

'In this weather, yes, it's the only way, otherwise I use the Land Rover to travel the moor. However, Prince still needs exercising, this way I can do both at once.'

'He's a magnificent animal,' she remarked, looking through a clearing patch of the windowpane to where the horse was tethered. 'Though I imagine your wife gets anxious when you're out riding in this weather.'

He glanced up quickly and set down his cup. 'Will you pour a cup for Martha?' he prompted, rising from his chair. 'I'll take it up now.'

Seeing his expression, Kate fell silent. It appeared she'd hit on a sensitive subject;

perhaps a wife didn't exist, or maybe had an accident whilst out riding?

During his absence from the kitchen, Kate reflected upon his expression when he'd replied to her question. Was it pain she'd seen in his grey eyes? And, if so, was it pain brought about by grief, or from bitterness? Surely, if he were not married he would quite simply have said so, wouldn't he?

With rising pique she sliced the bread more vigorously than intended. Ill-tempered creature, she fumed silently. Yet she had to admit he was a striking figure with his tall, good looks; lean and athletic with wind-tanned features, probably in his mid-thirties, but definitely grumpy.

It was when he returned to the kitchen that she noticed the scar. It ran under the edge of his jaw in a jagged line and though healing well, it had obviously been the result of a severe injury. Yet, when he gave a sudden smile, saying how pleased he was to find Martha looking so bright, it was hardly noticeable.

'I do believe she's improved already!' he declared, going back to stand before the brightly-burning fire. 'It will do her a power of good to have company. How long do you intend staying?'

'I'd have thought you would have discovered that by now,' she replied a trifle tartly. 'I noticed you already knew my name even though we've never been introduced.'

Compressing his lips, he strode over to the door, turning to face her as he remarked cryptically, 'I already know a great deal about you, young lady.'

In the doorway he turned to issue his final instructions, 'Don't forget to drop the latch, will you? And if you see any strangers snooping around let me know immediately.'

CHAPTER TWO

'Did you mention anything about me?' Kate asked Martha when she took up her breakfast tray. 'He knows my name, and he also made a very strange remark . . . said he knew more about me than I may be aware.'

'No, how could I? I hadn't laid eyes on him since I came home yesterday morning and I only had word of you coming when the District Nurse called.'

'Strange,' Kate muttered as she helped Martha into a more comfortable position.

Martha sighed happily as she set about the dainty portion of scrambled egg. 'Oh, it is good to be back . . . Hospitals are all right, but there's no place like home. And the doctor seems very pleased with my progress.'

'Yes, that's wonderful news. By the way, what is his name? He didn't bother to introduce himself when he arrived.'

'Alexander Blair. Took over the practice after his father died. Came back from Ireland—was with the army there. Won a medal, I believe . . .'

'Not for charm, I'm sure,' Kate returned under her breath.

'When you know him better you'll change your mind,' Martha chuckled.

'Even so, I hope I'm not taken ill whilst I'm here. By the way, is he married?'

'No, but I believe there was a woman in his life, though she doesn't appear to be around now. According to Annie Trousdale, his housekeeper, there was some trouble at his surgery—something went missing—I understand this woman was involved. He's never mentioned it, of course, and Annie's such an old gossip.'

'I see,' Kate murmured. 'Maybe that explains his attitude, he seems very bitter about something. I noticed a scar under his chin, I wonder how he got that.'

'Can't tell you, Kate, it must have happened whilst I've been ill.'

Although it was the last time the doctor's name came up in conversation that day, he persisted in entering Kate's thoughts. Assuming he would be keeping a professional eye on Martha's progress, she found herself wondering when his next call may be.

It was only when she was preparing for bed

that her thoughts came to dwell on Godfrey. And with a surge of relief she realised she hadn't for one moment been tempted to communicate with him. He knew her mobile telephone had recently been stolen, but she had sent him a message to say she had purchased a replacement before she left. So far, he had not bothered to enquire after her safe arrival, and she was determined not to be the first to ring.

Her father had suggested she widen her circle of friends, meet new people and not depend entirely upon Godfrey for either companionship or business contracts. She gave a short laugh; if he wanted her to widen her experience of life, then why on earth ask her to come here?

She was certain he had not been here for years, not since her mother died, and had arranged all improvements to the cottage by telephone. It was almost like being sent into seclusion; without Martha to care for life here would be unbearable.

She sighed and settled into the warm bed, but only minutes had passed before she heard the faint click of the metal door latch downstairs, and the sound of someone putting pressure on the door. Expecting it to be followed by a knock she reached for her dressing-gown and slid reluctantly from the bed.

Going to draw aside the heavy curtain she

slid open the window and peered down onto the snow-covered garden, noticing the gate was open. She called softly, 'Hello, who's there?' but got no response, and the almost eerie silence outside made her wonder if she had unknowingly drifted into sleep and dreamed it all.

But as she let the curtain fall back into place a dark shape caught her eye and she reached to switch off the reading lamp before taking another peep in time to see the dark figure dissolve into the shadow of the trees.

Convincing herself it was merely a trick of the light, yet slightly unnerved by the experience, she closed the window and latched it. She considered it best not to waken Martha, but should she mention it to the doctor as he had asked?

But however she tried to convince herself it was nothing to worry about, it was some time before sleep overcame her and it seemed like only minutes had passed when she was awakened by the sound of banging on the door downstairs.

Throwing back the bedclothes she darted over to the window to find the doctor staring up from the path below. Pushing her long hair back from her face she slid open the window and called, 'Will you wait a moment,' withdrawing quickly as a blast of cold air struck her bare shoulders. There was no escape from having to go and unbolt the door, so donning her dressing-gown she descended the stairs, surprised by the unexpected rise of excitement within her.

'Has someone called this morning?' he demanded to know, glancing back to the garden. 'I notice there are fresh footprints outside.'

Annoyed by his manner, she avoided mentioning the visitor of the previous evening. 'Of course. You're the first caller today, though it's an unearthly hour to call on anyone, least of all a patient who's most likely still asleep!' she accused him as he stepped over the threshold.

He stared at her in silence then glanced pointedly at his watch, surveying her critically from head to toe. 'It is precisely eight fifty-five,' he told her. 'We're early risers in these parts, whereas I expect you are used to rising much later.'

'Actually, you're wrong. However, it is no business of yours what time I choose to rise in the morning.'

'True,' he agreed with a shrug of his broad shoulders, 'I could have used the spare key, but now you keep it bolted I thought it may alarm you to hear someone trying to get in.' And crossing the kitchen he crouched before the hearth to strike a match and put it to the ready-laid sticks and paper.

'There's no need for you to do that, Doctor!' she said coolly. 'I can manage quite well on my own.'

'Even so, I detect a decidedly icy atmosphere in here,' he returned, rising to tower above her. 'No-one warned me of that!'

'Why should they, I'm not one of your patients!'

'I think Martha will have to take you in hand again,' he said with a hint of amusement. 'You're still young enough to learn.'

'Whatever my age, I don't need your advice, Doctor!' she exclaimed with a toss of her head. 'I'm not your patient, nor am I a child.'

'True, you are not my patient, but you are behaving like a child . . .'

'Let me inform you, I'm over twenty-one.'

'Which makes you old enough to be kissed,' he declared firmly. 'If only to silence you. 'And before she could protest, he took her firmly by the shoulders and pressed his mouth to hers in a gentle caress.

Later, as she relived those moments when he had held her in his arms, she let out a soft, despairing groan, realising the foolishness of allowing her thoughts to dwell upon this man. Rising to her feet she met her unsmiling reflection in the oak-framed mirror above the mantelshelf; perhaps she was missing Godfrey after all. She would telephone him as soon as the opportunity arose.

Having made that decision, she went up to collect Martha's lunch tray and ensure the heat in her bedroom was set at the right temperature so that she could enjoy a comfortable afternoon rest.

'You've neglected me this morning,' Martha grumbled. 'What on earth have you been doing down there?'

'Making sure the place is as tidy as you would expect,' Kate retorted good-naturedly.

'Don't you be overdoing that wrist of yours or it will never be right again, and you can't play the piano until it is.'

'It's fine now, Martha.'

'That's good! By the way, you didn't tell me what Doctor Alex said when you brought up my lunch. I was hoping I could go downstairs.'

'I didn't see him leave,' Kate explained a little awkwardly. 'He seemed in rather a hurry today.'

'Didn't he stay for a hot drink? He usually does on a morning such as this.'

'No, he did not,' Kate replied a trifle impatiently, 'I didn't invite him.'

Martha shot her a reproachful glance. 'He shouldn't have to wait for an invitation, my girl.'

Feeling like a thoroughly naughty child, Kate didn't wait to hear more, but went to her own room to change out of the clothes she'd worn to tackle the housework. She'd surprised herself to find she'd coped with tasks not so familiar to her without too much trouble, but felt more comfortable once she'd changed into a soft woollen dress, preparing for a quiet afternoon reading in front of the fire downstairs while Martha slept.

Curled up in a large, comfortable armchair beside the open fire, Kate opened her book, but she found it quite impossible to concentrate on the words written there. Instead, she found herself thinking of the doctor's next visit with almost pleasurable anticipation, though edged with a tinge of annoyance when she pictured his mocking dark eyes.

It was nearly an hour later, when she had almost drifted off to sleep in the comfort of the fire's glow that she realised someone was at the garden gate. Rising to her feet, she gave a sharp indrawn breath, seeing the chestnut hunter tethered beneath the shelter of the trees and the doctor striding down the path.

'You're a very lucky young lady,' he said pleasantly, removing his cap as he entered and crossed over to the fireplace.

'Why,' she feigned in equally pleasant tones, 'because you've chosen to call?'

'Now, now,' he chided softly, rubbing his hands together in front of the glowing fire, 'I mean your warm and comfortable situation. Actually, I came to ask if there is anything you require, as my groom has managed to bring a few supplies from the village. It's becoming much colder again.'

'Oh, I see,' she murmured with a rueful smile, 'it's very kind of you to concern yourself.

Actually, I brought quite a lot of provisions with me so I'm sure there's nothing we're likely to run short of for the next few days.'

His expression was serious as he straightened and turned in her direction. 'But that wasn't the main reason for my visit. I had a telephone call from your father.'

She frowned. 'My father rang you? I hadn't realised you were acquainted, it must be ages since he came up here.'

He nodded. 'He rang to enquire about Martha, and asked me to give you his love and tell you to enjoy your stay . . .'

'Thank you for bringing me the message. My mobile must have been switched off, and he'd know you would be calling on Martha.'

'Precisely! I'm the only medic around these parts, though he was better acquainted with my father . . .' He raised his hand to continue. 'Before I forget, there was something else. He said to tell you there are no letters or telephone messages but you are not to be too disappointed. He mentioned someone by the name of Downes, said you may have expected to hear from him.'

With a shrug she turned away. 'Godfrey Downes, yes, he was my agent.'

'Was? You make it sound as if your career has ended.'

'Maybe it has,' she said in a small voice, 'but I'd rather not talk about it.'

'As you wish, of course,' he said kindly,

'though that wrist injury shouldn't keep you away from the piano for much longer.'

About to remind him she had no wish to discuss the matter, she bit back her words. This man knew more about her than she felt comfortable with and he could well be the person her father had asked to keep an eye on her during her stay.

Suddenly aware he was regarding her with some concern, she picked up the poker and eased a smoking log further into the embers. 'Actually, my wrist doesn't trouble me at all so I expect I shall return to London as soon as Martha can manage on her own.'

'Not in this weather, I hope. Only a fool would risk it in these conditions.'

'Don't you think I realise that,' she countered with a toss of her head.

But when he saw tears fill her eyes, he said gently, 'Something's troubling you, Katherine, would you care to tell me about it.'

'I don't know what you mean,' she denied, averting her head as she brushed his hand aside.

'I think you do,' he contradicted softly. 'You're unhappy, I know.'

'Are you also a practising psychiatrist?' she shot at him with a lift of her chin. 'If so, I don't require your services.'

Compressing his lips into a firm line, he gave a groan of impatience. 'I always understood your father to say you were a pleasant-natured girl. But it seems he was wrong, you have a heart of ice.'

'Oh, I can be pleasant, in the right company,' she retorted airily.

'Which tells me exactly where I stand,' he said angrily.

'Why Martha insists on singing your praises I'll never know!' she threw at him.

He paused and turned to meet her defiant stare. 'Considering your father's such a gentleman, how he managed to raise such a spoiled brat is beyond me!' he spat out before closing the door behind him with rather more force than necessary.

Without looking back he mounted his horse and rode off in a flurry of snow as, striving to control her feelings, Kate went upstairs in response to Martha's call.

'What on earth is going on down there?' the older woman enquired, her face lined with concern. 'Such a heated exchange—I couldn't help but overhear.'

'Then you would hear him call me a spoiled brat!' Kate exclaimed angrily.

'After your rather nasty remark, I'm not surprised he retaliated,' Martha said with a slight shake of her head. 'What did you expect?'

'Even so, he has no right to speak to me that way.'

'Then perhaps you should try to be the daughter your father speaks about,' Martha said gently, though her expression was stern. 'You always were such a happy-go-lucky child, but I've noticed a change . . .'

'So he told me,' Kate interjected. 'My father must have gone into great detail about my character.'

'At least, it was complimentary,' Martha reminded her. 'And, if I'm not mistaken, there's something bothering you, my girl, it's unlike you to be sharp with anyone.'

'I, I'm sorry. It's just this . . . this awful weather,' she stumbled on. 'I'm not used to it, and . . .'

'And having to cope with looking after an old woman,' Martha put in. 'Not a very exciting prospect for any young person.'

'Oh no, nothing like that!' Kate protested quickly. 'I'm enjoying being with you, believe me, it's like old times. But that doctor of yours infuriates me.'

'You shouldn't let it bother you, Kate. After all, he may be the only one person we see for the next week—maybe more by the look of things outside.'

'As bad as that?' Kate sighed. 'Well, perhaps you are right, I have been a little touchy since my accident,' she excused herself. 'I'm sorry.'

'Don't apologise to me, Kate, he's the one who deserves that,' Martha said with a smile, and tilting her head to one side cajoled. 'I think you've found our Doctor Blair to be quite a challenge. You've noticed he's rather an attractive man and not merely a fuddy-duddy old country practitioner, after all.'

Down in the kitchen Kate gave a rueful smile as she prepared tea. Apologise to Doctor Blair? He would gloat over the humble position in which she placed herself. Better she avoid him, particularly if he was to bring up the subject of Godfrey again.

Satisfied with her decision, Kate took a tray laid for two up to Martha's room in preparation for a cosy chat by the bedroom fire. But she had no sooner placed the tray on the bedside table when there came a loud hammering on the door below.

'Don't tell me he's come back to preach again,' Kate moaned.

Martha shot her a glance of disapproval. 'Folk that know me usually come straight in, unless the door is locked.'

Kate's heart leapt. If she hadn't dropped the latch, why didn't the doctor walk straight in as usual, unless . . . could this be someone snooping round the place? 'Yes, I expect I have, I'd better go and see who it is.'

There came a second, and more impatient banging on the door as Kate ran down the stairs but, realising the caller may not be welcome, instead of opening the door she also slid the bolt home before calling, 'Who is it?'

A faint childish voice came from outside. 'It's David, David Bowman. My mother says will you get the doctor . . . please,' the boy ended on a pleading note.

A little warily, Kate slid back the bolt and opened the door to see a young lad with glowing red cheeks standing on the step. 'Are you alone?' she asked, peering out into the darkness. 'Is your mother ill?'

'No, Miss, it's my brother. Mum sent me to ask you to get Doctor Blair on your telephone.'

'You'd better come in, David. Where exactly do you live?'

'No, just up the road, not that far.'

'Well, I'm afraid our phone's not been reconnected since the last time the lines were down,' Kate said, indicating he should come indoors, 'but fortunately I've got my mobile.'

However, when she brought the mobile from her bedroom she was dismayed to find it had been left switched on and the battery needed charging.

'Oh no! That is infuriating, I'll also need to get a charger from town as I've left mine behind. I'll come with you and have a word with your mother. There may be something I can do to help.'

His young face lit up. 'Yes please, 'cos she hasn't anybody to help her since me dad died, only us kids.'

After a hurried word to Martha who suggested she take a torch, Kate slipped a scarf over her head and set off in the direction the young boy indicated.

Once inside the house, Kate began to realise the urgency of the errand. Across the low-beamed room a woman tended a moaning child who was lying on an ancient leatherette settee wrapped in blankets. She was mopping the youngster's brow, shaking her head from side to side, her expression one of deep despair. 'Is the doctor on his way?' she said anxiously. 'I do hope he won't be long?'

'I'm sorry, I couldn't get him, our phone, the one at Hawthorn Cottage, isn't working,' Kate said, venturing closer to the ailing child, 'but I'll go to the nearest public telephone . . .'

'The doctor was here this morning—usually calls to see if there is anything we need—but then I didn't know, Peter was fine.'

Becoming increasingly alarmed by the state of the child who appeared to be in agony, Kate pressed, 'Where's the nearest phone? I'll ask the doctor to come right away.'

'About half a mile down the road, past Hawthorn, near the little church by the wood . . .'

Without wasting another moment, Kate left the house to retrace her steps through the deep snow until she reached Hawthorn, where she called up to Martha to tell her where she was heading.

'Take good care,' she heard Martha call as she was leaving the house, remembering to slip the latchkey into her pocket.

'I will,' she replied brightly, her cheerful

response belying the trepidation she felt as she returned to the snowy tracks left by the doctor's horse.

She sped along the road as fast as she could until the telephone box loomed beside her, its interior in complete darkness.

As she entered the kiosk the snow began to fall heavily, and she gasped with relief when a clear male voice came on the line.

'I think you should come as quickly as possible,' Kate said after giving details of the child's symptoms through chattering teeth.

Obviously surprised to hear her speaking from a public telephone, he recovered quickly to ask, 'Who's with you?'

'No-one. The child looks so ill there was no other way. Our lines are down and my mobile is flat . . .'

'Can you make your way back to the house?' he cut in. 'And call on Martha as you pass Hawthorn, tell her what you're doing, and make sure you've locked the door.'

Facing the wind again, she pulled her scarf more tightly round her head to shield her from the heavily-falling snow. What help could she be to the doctor, she wondered? However prepared she was, she'd had only brief first-aid experience—most likely she'd faint!

She reached Hawthorn quite breathless from fighting against the strong wind that had blown the snow into drifts at the roadside, swirling it over the hedges like peaks of meringue. Unlocking the cottage door she merely called up to Martha, knowing every moment would add to the unbearable wait of Mrs Bowman who would be extremely relieved to know the doctor was on his way.

Shortly after leaving Hawthorn on her return to the Bowman's place, she heard a faint sound of hooves, dulled by the cushion of snow, and men's voices drawing nearer until horses and riders became visible through the curtain of white.

'Give me your hand, and step on my boot,' the doctor directed as he drew his mount to a slithering halt beside her. 'You can ride in front of me.'

'But I've not been on a horse for years,' she cried, 'particularly one as big as Prince.'

'Come along,' he demanded impatiently. And without wasting another second he slipped his foot down from the stirrup to make a step and gripping her firmly by the arm swung her effortlessly up on to the saddle before she had a chance to make further protest.

On reaching the house of the sick child the doctor drew his horse to a halt and leaned closer to say, 'It wasn't so bad, was it?' before he quickly dismounted and reached up to help her down, his strong hands almost spanning her waist.

Then, unhitching his medical case from behind the saddle, he turned to the other man whom he introduced as John, his groom, who gathered the reins of both animals and led them off to the shelter of the barn.

Hearing the sound of their voices as they approached the house, Mrs Bowman appeared in the doorway, clutching her apron with anxious hands.

'Thank goodness you're here, Doctor,' she breathed, ushering them inside. 'Peter's really bad now, I didn't know what to do.'

Doctor Blair slid a comforting arm round her weary shoulders as they approached the makeshift bed. 'Let's have a look at him, then.'

But, glancing towards the bed, even Kate could see the condition of the child had worsened since she left the house almost an hour before. To hide a wave of emotion she turned her attention to David.

'Don't worry,' she managed to whisper to the older child. 'Doctor Blair will soon have him well again.'

The doctor glanced up, his expression solemn as he spoke to the mother of the ailing child. 'We must get Peter to hospital as soon as possible, Mrs Bowman, I suspect he has acute appendicitis. He needs an operation.'

'My little Peter, in hospital!' she gasped.

'He's a very sick boy,' he intervened gently, 'but you'll be able to go with him. Katherine will look after David,' he ended, glancing up at Kate before reaching for his mobile phone to arrange for an ambulance to take the boy to hospital.

'But how will the ambulance get through?' Kate asked the groom.

'We use a helicopter in emergencies,' he told her. 'David and I will light beacons in the field nearby.'

'Can I help?' she offered. 'I feel so useless ...'

'You can make a pot of strong tea,' the doctor advised quickly. 'Mrs Bowman could do with one, and I'm sure she'll be glad of your company until I get back.'

Throwing off her fashionable, but very damp coat, Kate set to work, admiration for the doctor replacing any annoyance she had previously felt. He had a special kind of skill she realised as she filled the kettle from the brass tap over a shallow brown sink.

Her thoughts were interrupted when Mrs Bowman spoke. 'Would you really look after David?' she asked, her eyes still fastened on her sick child.

'Of course,' Kate assured her, 'and Martha would love him to stay with us.'

'Then I needn't worry about him,' she sighed thankfully. 'Doctor Alex was right, you're a sweet girl, and that's why I sent David to you for help.'

'The doctor said that?' Kate whispered in surprise as they settled down to drink the tea. 'I never expected ...'

She broke off at the sound of voices when

the men entered the room followed by David.

'Is the ambulance coming?' Mrs Bowman asked, for a moment hopeful until she saw the grave expression on the doctor's face.

Alex Blair shook his head, thoughtful for a moment before he announced the helicopter couldn't reach them until the approaching storm had abated. Kate's heart sank, until she saw him turn to Mrs Bowman to tell her of his intention in confident tones.

'It could be hours before the ambulance gets here, possibly tomorrow morning,' he said, his voice grave. 'So, rather than risk Peter's life, I've decided it best if I operate on him here.'

'Operate! Here?' the woman cried, raising her troubled eyes to his.

'I'm afraid so,' he agreed, giving her a brief smile, 'but I have John and Kate to assist me. You may rest assured I shall do everything possible for Peter.'

CHAPTER THREE

'You expect m-me to help?' Kate gasped and felt her heart lurch. 'But I've had no real training, no experience. I wouldn't know what to do . . .'

The doctor shot her an impatient glance. 'Don't worry, I'll give you instructions, and we'd better get started right away.'

Turning to Mrs Bowman he asked for a couple of clean cotton sheets and a large pan, then suggested perhaps it would be easier for her if she took David up to bed. For a moment the woman merely stared at him then, as though gathering her wits, began to follow his instructions.

Next, the doctor addressed his groom. 'Give me a lift with the dining-table, will you, John?'

'What do you want me to do?' Kate asked, determined to show him she wasn't completely useless, even though inwardly she quaked over what was to come.

'Find a bowl, soap, a nail brush and towels, then comfort young Peter until we're ready,' he instructed briskly as he and John placed the heavy oak table under the light, covering it with a folded blanket and the crisp white cotton sheets Mrs Bowman had provided.

Kate quickly obeyed, getting together the items he required before she went over to the settee where Peter lay, his little face contorted with pain. And as she spoke a few soothing words she was aware of the doctor comforting the child's mother, persuading her to leave. 'It shouldn't take too long,' he was saying gently, 'and then you can brew a pot of strong tea for us all. And maybe John can find a wee dram in his saddlebag,' he added with a chuckle.

Returning his attention to Kate and John, he gave instructions for the next stage. When the makeshift operating table was ready, the sterilising done, and they had scrubbed up thoroughly, Kate was provided with gloves and a cotton gown that reached down almost to her ankles.

'I do hope I can cope with this,' she wavered softly as she put her mask in place, 'I feel very nervous.'

Doctor Blair glanced up. 'I was under the impression you had done a little first aid in the past so don't tell me you're going to back out.'

'Of course I won't,' Kate returned, meeting the challenge in his eyes.

His only response was a flicker of a smile. With a syringe ready in his hand, but out of the boy's line of vision, he turned his attention to Peter to say gently, 'Now, Peter, just a little scratch and you won't feel that nasty pain any more.'

The doctor adjusted his mask and Peter was lifted on to the table. Kate watched as an airway was inserted then centred her attention on the doctor as he checked the anaesthetic and prepared to perform the operation.

'John has assisted me on a similar occasion once before,' he told her brightly, 'but I shall appreciate an extra pair of hands.'

'And did it go well?' she whispered, falling silent when she saw the concentration on his face.

'Perfectly—hardly a scar,' he replied cheerfully, without taking his eyes off his patient.

Kate felt more than a little apprehensive, her teeth were tightly clenched behind her mask and perspiration was beginning to dampen her brow. Only once did she glance down at the small incision, but had to look quickly away in case she may faint.

Yet, for some ridiculous reason, she was determined not to allow Alex Blair to observe any weakness on her part, particularly when he and John appeared totally calm.

Alexander Blair was the perfect man to have near in any crisis, she realised, her admiration for him increasing with every moment that passed.

To Kate it seemed an eternity before she heard his satisfied murmur as he again checked the child's pulse, though in reality it had been only a short time.

It wasn't took long before Peter began to rouse and his airway was removed. Doctor Blair spoke to him then turned to Kate to say, 'It's time to clear up now, then we'll call his mother and make good use of that boiling kettle.'

Mrs Bowman was tearfully relieved to see her son regaining consciousness. 'Oh, Doctor, I can't thank you enough,' she sobbed. 'I don't know what we'd have done if you hadn't come.'

'You can thank Kate for that,' he smiled. 'She's not a country girl, you know, but she got to the phone through a devil of a storm.'

Kate smilingly brushed aside Mrs Bowman's words of gratitude, but the doctor's remark annoyed her. Why must he keep on belittling townspeople, she fumed inwardly, casting him a cool glance.

Once everything had been cleared away and Peter made more comfortable on his makeshift bed, the rest of them settled down to the promised tea laced with whisky. Kate felt the life returning to her tired and aching body and realised the doctor must be quite exhausted.

He declared his intention to spend the night with Peter, enabling him to keep a constant check on the child's condition.

It was music to Kate's ears to hear Peter's steady breathing, interspersed with only the occasional sleepy whimper. It appeared the operation had gone well, and together with Mrs Bowman she felt a wave of admiration for the doctor's skill. However infuriating his manner could sometimes be, he inspired confidence, and both gratitude and trust glowed in Mrs Bowman's eyes.

'I must go up and tell David how his brother is,' she beamed.

'You finish your tea,' Alex Blair suggested kindly, indicating she return to her chair. 'Kate will keep an eye on Peter while I go and talk to David.'

As the doctor closed the door behind him,

Mrs Bowman turned to Kate. 'I do hope you'll come and see us again, Miss er . . .'

'Please, call me Kate,' she invited. 'And yes, I'd love to visit the boys, and if there's anything I can do to help please don't hesitate to ask.'

'Perhaps you wouldn't mind sitting with Peter while I feed the poultry for the next day or two. I'll not dare to leave his side, though David's a grand lad, and as he can't get to school until the weather improves, I shall have him home to help.'

'Does that mean the road to Elmsgarth is completely closed?' Kate said in surprise. 'Then we're totally isolated here!'

Mrs Bowman laughed. 'Happens often at this time of year—we're used to it—that's why Doctor Alex calls most days when folks can't get to the surgery.' She sighed, and glancing at the now sleeping child added thoughtfully, 'Aye, we owe a lot to Doctor Alex—tells me he performed a few emergency operations when he served his time in the army.'

'Will that be where he was injured? I noticed he has quite a nasty scar under his chin.'

'Can't say, he never talks about it. I only noticed it a couple of months ago, some time after he came back home to live,' the woman said. Then with a slight shake of her head continued, 'Aye, it would be grand to see him settled down, he's such a good doctor.'

Kate nodded. 'Yes, I can see he is, particularly in an emergency, but what exactly do you mean by settled down?'

'Well, he's not been the same since she left—her with the red hair. Always the same with his patients, mind you,' Mrs Bowman assured quickly, 'but it's no life for him in that great big house on his own.'

Kate's eyebrows lifted a little as she said, 'Oh, I thought he would have a family . . .' But before the other woman could respond she heard him coming down the stairs and hurriedly changed the subject. Smiling down at the child she remarked, 'Peter seemed very peaceful now.'

'David's fallen asleep,' he told them as he entered the warm room, 'So I suggest you get some rest Mrs Bowman. I'll call you early in the morning. Peter should be quite stable by then.'

'But Doctor, I can't leave you to see to him, you must be in tatters . . .' Mrs Bowman objected in her strong local accent.

'Of course you can, you'll have a long day tomorrow,' he interrupted with a smile. 'Don't worry, Kate will keep me company for a while.'

Kate looked up in surprise. 'Perhaps Martha will wonder where I am,' she ventured after Mrs Bowman retired. 'Not that I object to staying, but I don't want to worry her unnecessarily.'

'Relax. Once I realised the seriousness of

the situation, I suggested John let her know what has happened on his way back. In any case, I wanted an opportunity to speak to you.'

'But how will he get in? I have the key here in my pocket.'

Alex laughed. 'Don't worry, he'll get the spare. You see, we had a copy made—but that was before we knew you were coming. Your father didn't ring me until the evening you arrived.' His expression grew more serious as he continued, 'Actually, it is about Martha I'd like to have a word.'

Kate relented and returned to her chair by Peter's bed. 'There's nothing wrong, is there?' she whispered. 'I mean, Martha is going to get better?'

'Relax now, it's nothing quite so serious as you appear to expect. What concerns me more is how long you will be able to stay with her—her recovery will take time, six to eight weeks at least.'

'At least!' Kate gasped, then glancing quickly to where Peter lay continued in a lowered voice, 'But I can't possibly stay here that long. I've got to get back to rehearsals. I can't live off my father indefinitely.'

'I don't think that will trouble your father—he's quite happy for you to be here.'

'Oh yes, of course, I had forgotten, you and he appear to be making all my decisions of which I am not expected to question.'

'Kate, really,' he admonished with a flicker

of a smile. 'I admire your father. He only wants the best in life for you, I know.'

'You know,' she echoed softly with a shake of her head. 'Why did you not tell me you and he were so well acquainted when first we met?'

'You hardly gave this gout-ridden old country squire an opportunity, remember?' he countered with a wry smile. 'However, it is Martha who concerns me just now, she is going to need someone to care for her for some time yet.'

'Then, how long before she's well enough to travel?' Kate asked. 'I don't mean to sound heartless, but it would be easier if I could take her back to London to convalesce.'

'She'd hate that and you know it,' he responded sharply. 'In any case, what is so important that means you must rush back south?'

'My future, I suppose,' she admitted, and now when she thought of London and her career she felt an urge to make contact with Godfrey. What was Godfrey doing now?

'Something wrong?' he queried with an expression of concern.

'No, well nothing you can do anything about,' she returned quickly. 'It's just that I didn't expect to be here for much more than a couple of weeks.'

'That is better than nothing, I suppose,' he responded, causing her a pang of guilt. 'And I appreciate you being here tonight as I don't think Mrs Bowman could have coped. She would be too anxious, naturally. As it is, Peter's not out of danger yet. I'm not quite as well equipped as they are at the district hospital and there's always the risk of infection.'

'But you do think he'll be all right, don't you, Doctor?' Kate asked worriedly. 'You seemed quite pleased with him earlier.'

'Didn't want to worry his mother unnecessarily, she needed her rest. I will call her should there be a change in the boy's condition.'

He rose and went to check his patient's pulse once more and appeared satisfied. Returning to his chair he leaned forward, his hand resting briefly on her arm as he said, 'By the way, Kate, I'd prefer it if we were less formal. Please, call me Alex.'

'All right, Alex,' she murmured then, unsure of how to react, gestured to where his patient lay to ask, 'Can I do anything to help?'

'No, it may be wiser for you to go. I'd like to walk you back to Hawthorn but I can't possibly leave the boy . . .'

'Don't worry, I'll be fine,' she broke in to assure him.

Reaching for her coat that had been spread out to dry over the back of a chair, he held it out while she slid her arms down the sleeves. As she fastened the buttons he turned up the collar and tucked it round her neck. 'Thank you so much, Kate,' he said softly, his hands still on her collar as he added, 'I would welcome someone as capable as you to assist me, permanently,' before dropping a swift kiss on her forehead and turning her towards the door.

Pushing aside her fur-lined hood she glanced back to see Alex faintly outlined in the light from the cottage porch. But in only a moment or two the visibility decreased with the falling snow, obliterating him from sight.

'Alex—Alexander,' she murmured to herself. The name suited him and she repeated it once or twice, a smile on her lips as she trudged along until she saw a faint light from Hawthorn cottage ahead. As she drew nearer to the house she had difficulty negotiating the side of the road.

Deep drifts of snow had formed where the wind had found gaps in the hedge and it fell into the top of her boots which by now were soaking wet.

At the cottage, she paused a while before going indoors, turning back to face the way she had come. But there wasn't a sign of the house now, no glow of light, no Alex, only an eerie whiteness separating them. In the total silence she became more aware of the beating of her heart, and she drew off a glove to touch her brow where Alex's lips had briefly rested.

It had been a gentle kiss, nothing like the last time when he had taken her completely by surprise. Her heart jolted almost painfully as she recalled that first kiss.

Reproaching herself for allowing her thoughts to dwell on the local doctor, she swung round to go indoors. She put her present feelings down to the emotional atmosphere of the evening when an ailing child had been saved in circumstances normally considered impossible.

Telling herself she'd gone a little soft in the head, she knocked the snow off her boots and went indoors. True, Alex Blair was a good doctor, but he was a lonely man, Mrs Bowman had said, though could his loneliness be of his own making?

'Is that you, Kate?' she heard as she took off her coat and spread it over the clothes horse to dry.

'Yes, I'll be up in a moment,' Kate replied, taking the poker to try and rouse the dying embers in the grate, 'but first I'll make us a hot drink.'

Taking two mugs of hot chocolate upstairs, Kate made herself comfortable on Martha's bed and began to relate all that had happened that evening.

'I'm sure it can't have been easy for you, whereas John will have experienced something of the kind before.'

'Glad I didn't faint, he wouldn't have let me forget it,' Kate said, wiggling her cold toes in the ends of her damp socks.

Martha clicked her tongue. 'Come now, I'm sure he appreciated your help—he wouldn't expect more from someone unqualified. John said you were very brave.'

'He seems to have the impression all townspeople are weak and stupid,' Kate persisted.

Martha gave her an indulgent smile. 'Never mind, I think you did extremely well, and I have every confidence in Peter pulling through after Doctor Alex treated him.' Her eyes travelled to the ceiling, gazing thoughtfully into space as she murmured, 'Aye, he's a fine man—staying with the child through the night—not many would do that . . .' Martha's voice faded to a whisper as she relaxed on her pillows, relieved to know all was well.

Gently taking the cup from Martha's hand, Kate went quietly from the room. The tension of the evening, coupled with the warmth of the cottage after the cold walk back soon had her seeking the comfort of her bed.

The following morning, Kate had just finished breakfast when she heard the dull sound of hoofbeats. Rising in anticipation, she already had the door open when Alex strode down the path.

'Is Peter all right?' she blurted out before Alex reached the house. 'How is he this morning?'

'Hey, one question at a time!' he smiled, kicking his riding boots against the scraper before entering. And standing before the fire he told her, 'Peter's fine. I'm just on my way back there now.'

'Then you've been home?'

'Yes, John got in touch with Miss Garbutt. She's the retired district nurse who helps me out occasionally, and she was only too happy to sit with Peter whilst I go out on my rounds.'

'But you haven't had any rest, have you?'

He ran a hand over his chin and grinned. 'Do I look so bad? Actually, I had no time, Miss Garbutt came just after seven so I made a number of calls on my way home.'

'You must be awfully tired,' Kate sympathised and went on to enquire further on Peter's progress.

'I expect I dozed a little,' Alex confessed, 'but Peter came through the night without any trouble.'

'Is there anything I can do to help?' Kate offered. 'I know I'm not a nurse but I'd be more than willing.'

'That is thoughtful of you, Kate. When he's over the worst, I'm sure his mother would be delighted to have you call.'

'Yes, I intend to, but won't he be going into hospital?'

'By the look of it, there's no chance of an ambulance getting through for another day or two and by then, hopefully, he'll be showing signs of recovery.' He paused to smile at her, saying, 'As for you, Katherine, not being a nurse didn't prevent you from assisting me last evening, and you didn't object to helping with the clearing up so that John could get away in case of further calls.'

'Do you live alone—is there no-one else to take the calls?'

His expression changed. 'Yes, I live alone, entirely by choice,' he said.

'But that is no help in an emergency,' she reminded him, unable to resist adding, 'Especially with only a Londoner to rely upon.'

'I suppose I deserve that,' he conceded with a rueful smile.

Kate turned away from his disturbing gaze suddenly very aware of the totally masculine quality of his every movement and tone. Fearing the colour in her cheeks would give her away she busied herself at the sink and quelled the unreasonable urge to ask him to leave.

'What's wrong, Kate?' he asked gently. 'Were you upset by my small demonstration of gratitude when you left last night?'

'Of course not, that's ridiculous . . .' she responded a trifle too quickly.

'Are you missing London, your friends . . . maybe a special friend?' he probed, watching her reaction as he spoke.

'Yes, maybe I am . . .' she murmured, unaware that his jaw had hardened as he returned his cup and saucer to the table.

'Then perhaps I should go, but if you must

persist on wasting your young life on that worthless creature in London, well . . . words fail me . . .'

For a moment she was speechless. 'What I choose to do with my life is my business!' she managed at last. 'So please, just leave.'

His mouth became a thin line, and snatching up his tweed cap he said coolly, 'Certainly, as soon as I have completed my professional duties here—the sole reason for my visit.'

Her father shouldn't have divulged details of her private life to someone who was a stranger to her. And yet, did it really matter what Alex Blair knew about her? It was unlikely they would meet again once she had returned to London. It was very confusing.

To her annoyance, from upstairs came the sound of laughter, and then she heard Martha join in. During the time she spent with his patient, Kate wondered if she had come into their conversation. Something had amused them both, so as soon as she heard him leave she immediately went up to Martha's room.

'You two were having a good laugh,' she remarked casually as she flicked a duster over the dressing table.

'Oh yes, he brightens my day,' Martha agreed, chuckling afresh.

Kate forced a laugh. 'I hope he wasn't talking about me,' she said, glancing in the mirror to catch the reflection of Martha in her bed.

Martha gave a wry smile. 'No, dear, except praise for what you did up at the Bowman's place last evening. But I didn't hear any laughter from you downstairs. In fact, I notice you are rather touchy where Doctor Alex is concerned.'

'Nothing to laugh about,' Kate replied, attempting a casual air. 'As a matter of fact, he can be quite irritating.'

'Pity, he'd enjoyed your company, particularly after what you did to help.'

'Don't worry, he thanked me, and I understand Peter had quite a good night.' Kate conceded, hurriedly changing the subject. 'I can't get the car out yet so I may take a walk up there later to allow Mrs Bowman a break.'

'Good idea,' Martha agreed. 'Doctor told me old Nurse Garbutt will be calling on me this afternoon. She usually likes to stay and chat for an hour or two so I'll be all right if you want to go, she'll use the spare key.'

CHAPTER FOUR

Fortunately, it had stopped snowing by the time Kate set off for the Bowmans' home although it was extremely cold outside. She was wearing a pair of Martha's fur-lined boots with an extra pair of thick socks inside; hardly the most fashionable footwear, but she considered her appearance didn't matter quite so much in weather like this. She had promised to be back before darkness fell as more snow was forecast for later in the day.

'It's so good of you to come,' Mrs Bowman greeted her.

Both the Bowman boys were pleased to see her, though Peter seemed a little sleepy still. 'What would you like to do?' Kate asked, seating herself beside the folding bed in which Peter lay.

'Will you tell us a story?' David replied eagerly.

Mrs Bowman was able to get on with her chores whilst Kate read stories to two contented youngsters until their mother announced she was about to brew a pot of tea. It was as she drank the tea and ate a delicious home-made scone that Kate noticed it was already beginning to grow dark.

'Perhaps I ought to be getting back to Hawthorn,' she said, setting down her cup. 'The nurse was calling on Martha this afternoon but I don't want to delay her for too long.'

Mrs Bowman nodded. 'She's coming to sit with Peter tonight, Doctor Alex arranged it. He's been back a few times since breakfast, and he's calling to check on him this evening, though I don't expect him to stay over again as he'll have other folk to attend to.'

'But how does the nurse manage to get around, does she also ride horseback?'

Mrs Bowman laughed. 'No, I think our old nurse is a bit too hefty for that, but she doesn't live far away—her brother brings her over the top field by tractor.'

Kate smiled. 'Quite an efficient arrangement,' she said, 'perhaps I should get one, as my little car is useless in this weather.'

'Call on us whenever you like, I know the boys will be glad to see you.'

Kate was getting quite used to trudging through the snow and followed the track that had been cut into the deep drifts giving the effect of a narrow passage in places. Martha had told her the local farmers and their workers did this to make it a bit easier for the locals.

It was the stillness she noticed the most as she pushed on in the now eerie light into the shadows of the trees that grew near Hawthorn. But as she drew closer to the cottage gate she was startled to see a tall figure climbing over the boundary fence about thirty yards further along. She came to a sudden halt, causing her feet to shoot from beneath her and she fell back into the deeper snow.

Struggling to her feet she gasped a shaky 'Hello!' But there was no response from the man who was hurrying away in the opposite direction.

Puzzled, she stayed where she was for a few

moments, listening for the type of transport he was using. But why hadn't he responded to her call instead of rushing away?

She decided it best not to mention the man she'd seen leaving, but Martha surprised her by saying she'd had a caller whilst Kate was out. 'I didn't see him myself as I'd just got back into bed,' she said, 'it was Nurse Garbutt who spotted him in the garden.'

'What time was this?' Kate asked.

'Oh, about half-an-hour ago, not long before Nurse Garbutt left.'

'What did he want?' asked Kate, assuming this was the same man she had spotted leaving the garden only minutes ago.

'Well, he told Nurse Garbutt he was a distant relation of mine, a nephew or something like that, on a visit from Australia, he said. But I can't recall any relative of mine living in that faraway country . . .'

'And you say you haven't a relative in Australia?'

Martha shook her head. 'No, no-one that I can recall.'

'But he didn't leave his name or say when he intended to call again,' Kate murmured thoughtfully. 'Seems very strange to me.'

'Nurse Garbutt assumed he'd got the wrong house, that's what it was.'

'Mmm, she could be right,' Kate agreed, not wishing to alarm Martha, yet the more she thought about it, the more convinced she was that this man's visit was not as innocent as Martha or the nurse assumed it to be.

'Now tell me, Kate, how is the Bowman child today?'

'Oh, Peter was quite restful considering what he'd been through. And I understand the doctor has called two or three times today.'

'Nurse Garbutt tells me she is going to sit with him overnight to allow his mother to get her proper rest,' said Martha. 'She's one of the old school you know, and very reliable. Will you go and see Peter tomorrow?'

'Is the nurse coming here again?'

Martha shook her head. 'The poor dear will be tired out, she'll need her rest, but I'm quite able to be left, though I would appreciate a hand to get out of bed before you go. Providing my walking stick is within reach, there is no need for you to stay with me all the time.'

'Maybe, but I'd rather someone was here to keep you company . . .'

Much as she wanted to spend time with Peter Bowman, Kate didn't feel she could leave Martha alone until the mystery caller could be accounted for. She should mention the visit to Alex Blair, or would he consider she was making an unnecessary fuss? Maybe she would mention it to her father, as the caller could already be known to him. It was then that she remembered she must get the charger for her mobile phone, so she asked to borrow Alex's groom, John's.

Kate expected him that evening, so when there came a knock on the door she unlocked it.

'Doctor Alex asked me to tell you about his visits to Miss Cussons while I was dropping off my charger,' John explained as he knocked the snow from his boots and stepped over the threshold. 'As this house phone has not yet been connected he wants me to take down the number of your mobile so that he can contact you. You see, he'll be attending the child up at the farm more regularly during the next few days, so it'll help if he can check with you how Miss Cussons is faring.'

'Of course, it's freezing outside, John, come in to the kitchen?'

'Thank you.' He indicated the gently-burning fire and turned to her to say, 'I see you've been out to the wood shed. I could have brought the logs in for you if I'd known.'

She gave him a blank look. 'No, I haven't actually . . .'

'Oh, I see, I noticed footprints near the shed so assumed you'd been out there.'

'Then it must have been Nurse Garbutt. I must admit, bringing in more fuel had completely slipped my mind. But we do have other heaters, both down here and in the bedrooms so we wouldn't freeze.'

He grinned. 'It's not like old Nurse Garbutt to do a favour like that, she must have taken a liking to you.'

She glanced to the large basket in the alcove and laughed. 'Don't worry, I stocked up well yesterday so it's not a problem,' Kate said, and admitted, 'I hadn't a clue as to how much we would use each day.'

'That wood's hard, but once you get it going it'll burn for hours,' he told her. 'And when you need stocking up you know what to do. I pass here most days.'

'That's very kind of you, John, but I'm sure you already have enough to do for the doctor. Incidentally, how many staff does he have in the practice?'

'Apart from his partner, and a semi-retired lady doctor, he's on his own. His partner does a round on the other side of Elmsgarth, and the lady covers surgery appointments when Doctor Blair or his partner have a day off.'

'Not a lot for an area this size, is it?' she commented. 'He must have a great deal of help at home to enable him to work so hard.'

'Only Mrs Trousdale and her daughter, they do the cooking, washing and cleaning—have done for years. I do the shopping and outdoor chores, see to the horses, and give a hand with anything else when required.'

'But what about the surgery—appointments, telephone calls, that kind of thing—surely you don't do that as well? He'll need to have a receptionist.'

John drew in a wary breath. 'He did,' he

told her after a moment, 'but that's a taboo subject, I'm afraid. I'm surprised Miss Cussons hasn't mentioned it, she's sure to know. However, after she left . . .'

'She—the receptionist?'

He avoided replying and continued, 'After that Doctor Blair managed to solve the problem by persuading his partner's wife to take on the job once their youngest had started school. You see, it's not easy to get staff to work in these remote places, particularly with the soaring price of property. And now I hear his partner's wife is expecting another baby so I don't know what he'll do.'

Who was the taboo subject, Kate wondered?

'I'd better be getting back to Ivy Lodge,' John said.

After John had left, Kate couldn't wait to go up and ask Martha to explain the mystery surrounding Alex Blair's receptionist. She quickly made a plate of dainty sandwiches for her and a more substantial one for herself and, along with cups of hot chocolate, loaded them on to a tray and carried it upstairs.

'Ah, that looks nice!' Martha exclaimed with a smile. 'I was beginning to feel a little peckish.'

'Actually, I would have brought it up a while ago but John called to bring a mobile phone charger.'

'Mmm, it could be useful until we get our

own line connected again. I was told the wires had been damaged, but accidentally or intentionally, I'm not sure.'

'Ah well, that's another reason why I wouldn't leave you entirely alone. Supposing you need something and no-one is here.'

'Well, if you want to visit the Bowman boy you could always leave that mobile thing of yours with me—that is, if you show me how to use it. I know his mother would be glad of a break.'

'I suppose I could,' Kate agreed after a moment's hesitation. 'Mrs Bowman said she would appreciate me going as it'll allow her to attend to the outside duties, though whilst David's not at school I expect he'll give a hand.'

'I'll be fine,' Martha insisted. 'This heater your father had installed for me last year is marvellous—no carrying coal upstairs these days—and now we have the television I don't mind being confined to my bedroom.'

Kate smiled. 'Good, so I'll show you how to use the mobile before I go then you won't feel so cut off.'

'I hope I can manage it, I'm not used to such new-fangled things.'

'Anyway, it's only in case of an emergency, I can pre-set it, and if I'm away only a short time you're unlikely to need it.'

Kate was about to broach the matter of the mystery connected with Alex Blair that John had mentioned, but Martha cut her short to ask if her father was likely to telephone soon.

'I'd like you to thank him for all he's done,' she said, 'and you can tell him I'm fine, apart from the heavy snow there's been no trouble.'

'If he rings you can tell him yourself,' Kate said, 'but what is all this about trouble? Were you anticipating problems?'

'No, no, of course not,' Martha denied, rather too quickly Kate thought.

'And what is this secret regarding Doctor Blair's staff?' she broke in.

Martha eyed her keenly. 'Who's been gossiping to you—Mrs Bowman?'

'No, just a feeling I had, but why the mystery?'

'Don't let it bother your pretty little head,' Martha said firmly. 'If Doctor Alex wants you to know then he'll tell you himself.'

The following day, Kate decided to call on Peter Bowman before lunch leaving Martha a flask of soup to keep her going until she got back. The snow was crisp and deep, though there hadn't been another fall overnight. It was bitterly cold.

As she stepped out, as briskly as the hard-packed snow would allow, she thought about the man who had come to the cottage the evening before and considered the reason he had given for being there.

She hoped her father would telephone after she got back when she could ask if he had an explanation and could the story of being Martha's long-lost relative be true. To her knowledge, it was because he believed Martha to be without any family connections that he had persuaded her to live in Hawthorn Cottage rent-free.

Not that she was without money, he had told Kate, he knew her sister had bequeathed her a tidy sum, but if she wanted to leave it to a children's charity, who was he to object.

Kate frowned slightly as she reflected upon Martha saying the telephone wires had been damaged. Intentionally damaged or not, it was fortunate she had charged the battery of her mobile, she realised and wondered suddenly if Godfrey had tried to contact her. She would check on her return.

Entering the Bowman's house, she found young Peter propped up on pillows. His delighted mother thanked her for coming then went out to join her eldest son who was working in the farm buildings.

'Did you know about them being burgled?' Peter said as Kate reached for a book and seated herself beside his bed.

'Who's been burgled?' she asked, faintly alarmed by the child's blunt statement.

'Them post people—the old ones that live at the Manor near Elmsgarth,' he told her, his blue eyes wide from the excitement of relating his story. 'And their telephone wires had been cut.'

‘Telephone wires!’ Kate echoed, then quickly collected her thoughts to add, ‘Oh, what a shame. I do hope they are all right.’

His expression more serious, he went on to say, ‘My mam says they have a lot of money, but I hope they don’t come an’ rob us or we’ll have nothing left.’

‘I shouldn’t think so, Peter, we are too far away . . .’

‘Doctor Alex had warned them,’ he broke in to announce, ‘I heard him talking to Mam this morning.’

‘Oh well, he’ll make sure they are all right,’ she consoled, then queried, ‘So the doctor has already been to see you today?’

‘Yeah, and Nurse Garbutt was here until Mam came down. We had a fire lit all night!’

She smiled. ‘And you are feeling much better today, I see.’

He wrinkled his nose as he told her, ‘My tummy’s a bit sore where the doctor was sewing me, but he says it will soon get better now the bad bit is out.’

‘I understand there may be another fall of snow so perhaps I ought to go,’ she said when Mrs Bowman came back indoors an hour later. ‘All being well, I’ll be back tomorrow. If that is all right with you?’

‘You’re more than welcome.’ The woman smiled. ‘I expect Doctor Alex will be back this afternoon, and still on horseback if we get another fall.’

Kate covered the journey back to Hawthorn reasonably quickly and found herself thinking of Alex Blair most of the way.

Finding Martha sitting upright in bed with the mobile clutched in her hand she asked, 'Have we had a call?'

'No, not yet, I just thought I'd be ready for it when it rang.'

Kate started to giggle. 'You don't have to press the button on the first ring,' she said. 'Why not leave it on your bedside table.'

'But it's so small I can't imagine much sound coming out of it. I may not be able to hear who's speaking so I'd rather you keep it in your pocket.'

'But you didn't need to use it?' Kate queried, striving to contain her laughter as she slipped the item in question into the pocket of her jeans.

'No, but I'm certain I heard someone knocking on the door a half an hour ago. It can't have been Doctor Alex or the nurse, they would have let themselves in.'

Kate looked thoughtful, then turned to go downstairs. Could the caller have been the same dark-coated figure she had seen the previous day?

Down in the kitchen she turned on the cooker ready to start cooking the meal, frowning as she still puzzled over who the caller could have been, when the phone in her pocket gave its familiar ring.

Thinking it may be her father she gave him a cheerful welcome, but it was not his voice she heard in reply but the rather stern tones of Alex Blair.

'You were out this morning?' he said, his tone faintly accusing.

'Yes, I went to see Peter but I was away only a little over an hour,' she explained. 'Martha was fine, I left her my mobile . . .'

'But you took the key!'

Slightly taken aback by his tone she retaliated crossly, 'Of course I did, otherwise how would you expect me to get back in?'

'No, the other key,' he said with a hint of impatience. 'John called with fresh milk but he got no reply, nor could he get in. Why have you removed the spare key from the shed?'

'I haven't removed a key from anywhere!' she said indignantly. 'In fact, I didn't even know there was a spare in the shed . . .'

'Ah, so Martha didn't tell you,' he interrupted. 'Then perhaps I should explain . . . You see, before I heard you were coming to Hawthorn, I had to think of some way of making calls on Martha. Also there was the nurse to consider and John delivering food so we had to gain entry somehow. I didn't want Martha having a fall on the stairs if she came down to let us in so there was no other way.

'Naturally, John was most concerned this morning when he found no sign of the key anywhere, and he'd noticed footprints near the shed so he presumed you had removed it.'

'I see, so you didn't prefer to carry the key on you?'

'No, it was more convenient for us all if it was at the house.'

'Actually, Martha had heard someone knocking, and I must confess I did wonder who it could have been as we'd had a caller yesterday whilst I was visiting the Bowman's.'

'Say that again, Kate. You had a caller yesterday? At what time was this?'

'It must have been half past three—or thereabouts—before Nurse Garbutt left. I got back around four but she'd already gone. He told the nurse . . .'

'Did he give his name?' he interrupted. 'What did he want?'

'I'm trying to tell you, he told the nurse he was a nephew of Martha's but we think he came to the wrong house . . .'

'She has no relatives. You see, I needed the name of her next of kin for my records and she gave your father's.'

'How strange,' Kate murmured. 'If he calls again I'll ask him to explain.'

'No,' he rapped out. 'If he comes anywhere near Hawthorn you must ring me immediately. I'll deal with him—understand?'

Hearing the concern in Alex's voice immediately had a calming effect. She was sure the mystery would be easily solved when the nurse discovered she had inadvertently slipped the key into her pocket.

CHAPTER FIVE

Kate's father telephoned early that evening, and when she mentioned the supposed relative of Martha's, he assured her it was unlikely such a person existed.

'Martha had only one sister and she never married.'

'Even so, it's rather worrying, though should he turn up here again I'll tell him where to go,' Kate said.

'Much simpler than that, don't open the door to him and call the police, or Alex Blair. Promise me you will?'

'Actually, that is what your doctor friend advises—or rather, demands I do.'

He chuckled. 'Keeps you in line, does he?'

'Thinks he can!' she said with a short laugh. 'He doesn't give me credit for any intelligence, and then I discover you and he are friends.'

'Actually, I knew his father better. Alex was abroad when your mother and I used to spend time at the cottage. Even so, it's good to know you have someone up there you can turn to should there be a problem.'

They continued to chat about Martha's improving state of health, and how they were coping in the present weather conditions. She enjoyed talking to him but noticed how he paused when she asked if Godfrey had been in touch with her London address when he'd last been home.

'I'm sorry, darling, but you are worth better than such as he . . .' he said bluntly.

'But my career,' she broke in. 'He promised he would have a contract lined up for me with one of London's top orchestras so I must know when it is likely to be. You see, I understand Martha is going to need help for some time yet, but as there's no piano here I shall soon be out of practice.'

'There's no hurry,' her father soothed. 'I'll get you a piano as soon as it can be arranged. Give yourself time, you've been at Hawthorn barely a week.'

'Mmm, I suppose you're right, but I'm surprised Godfrey hasn't tried to contact me. I had thought of ringing him but I know he refuses to take calls, and he hates to be disturbed when he's busy.'

'Busy, pah! If you remember, Kate, your dear mother never had a very high opinion of him, and usually she was right.'

'Yes, I suppose so,' she responded woefully, recalling her mother's cool but polite welcome of Godfrey when she had first introduced them almost four years ago.

But Kate was impatient. Shortly after her father went off the line she keyed in Godfrey's office number. Hearing no response she tried his London apartment and had to leave a message on his answerphone urging him to ring her back.

*   *   *

The weather seemed to be easing a little when Kate got up the following morning.

'Martha, I do believe it is thawing!' she exclaimed excitedly when she took up her breakfast. 'Soon I can drive down to Elmsgarth, do a bit of shopping. I'll buy Peter a colouring book, but first I must check the car will start.'

'Yes, I expect being confined up here has been hard on you, but when the conditions improve you'll love it. The moor is a picture in fine weather and it won't be long before you see a few lambs frolicking about.'

Kate gave her a quick smile but silently wondered if she would still be here when the lambs were born. How long would it be before Martha became fully mobile and she could return to London? Nurse Garbutt had mentioned getting Martha downstairs, but at present she was kept busy at the Bowman's place until Peter regained his health.

As she ate her own breakfast, Kate's thoughts returned to London and her career, but before she had time to consider it further she heard a vehicle draw up outside and saw Alex Blair heading towards the house.

‘Good, I’m pleased to find you are keeping it bolted,’ he said as she opened the door to him. ‘I managed to get the Land Rover out today so I thought I’d give you a call.’

‘Will you join me?’ she offered, indicating the breakfast table. ‘I don’t know if you’ve already eaten, if not I can prepare something.’

He smiled down at her. ‘Actually, I had breakfast earlier, but that coffee smells good, if you have a cup to spare.’

‘Yes, there’s a pot-full. Take a seat and help yourself,’ she invited, delighted to see him. ‘Oh, by the way, had the nurse taken the key away by mistake?’

He shook his head and took a sip of coffee before replying. ‘Unfortunately no, which is another reason for me being here. John, the nurse, and myself are the only ones who knew where the key was, and neither she nor John have removed it. It seems the nurse was the last person to use it when she called on Martha the day after Peter’s operation, and she insists she put it back in its place.’

Kate sighed. ‘I can’t explain it. As I told you, I wasn’t aware it was there.’

‘Then it was either spotted accidentally, or someone has been watching this place,’ he suggested, his expression grave. ‘But the question is, who?’

‘I’ve not seen anyone, that is apart from the man who was still hanging around after the nurse was here . . .’

'Hanging around!' he exclaimed, rising from his chair to loom over her. 'You never mentioned this before!'

'Yes, I did. I told you about the man who called, the one who claimed to be a relative,' she said indignantly, drawing back in her chair. 'I assumed the man I saw when I got back was the same person the nurse had spoken to, though she said she'd left half an hour earlier.'

Alex Blair compressed his lips thoughtfully and returned to his seat. 'I think you'd better tell me all you know about this fellow, and describe him if you can,' he said after a moment. 'Obviously Nurse Garbutt had not suspected anything as she didn't mention it to me.'

'Nurse Garbutt assumed he had come to the wrong house,' Kate told him and went on to relate what she'd heard about the stranger. 'But why would he be here at all? Even if he is a relative, it's most unlikely he would call without a previous arrangement, particularly in these conditions.'

'Did you noticed what transport he used, Kate? Did you see a four-wheel drive of some kind—you know, like the one I'm driving today?'

'No, I didn't, and I remember wondering how he came to be here as I couldn't see a vehicle, unless he'd left it some distance from the house.'

'He must have had a reason for that,' Alex

remarked with a gentle shake of his head. 'It's all very mysterious.'

She gave him a questioning glance, silent for a moment as she gathered courage to say quietly, 'But it is not the only mystery around these parts, is it, Alex? There is something about your own situation I don't understand, and nobody seems willing to enlighten me.'

She held his gaze, watching for any reaction in his dark eyes. 'You shouldn't listen to idle gossip.'

'I am not in the habit of gossiping,' she flung back. 'But you must admit you are inclined to shut people out—well, me anyway. Of course, I can appreciate your profession will have its problems,' she rushed on to add with concern with her voice, 'though I have a feeling it is something more personal. If I can help in any way . . .'

She saw a faint smile on his lips, and he reached out to cover her hand where it lay on the table, tightening his hand on hers when he felt her try to draw away. 'You know, Kate, you are surprisingly perceptive for one so young, and blessed with the sensitivity of someone quite mature . . . in years, that is,' he hastened to add.

She gave a short laugh. 'Thank you for the compliment, though I'm not sure I deserve it. However, whatever is bothering you, if you want to talk about it . . . it's up to you. I promise it wouldn't go any further.'

'Thank you, Kate, I value your sincerity,' he murmured, raising her hand to his lips to place upon it the briefest of kisses. He then gave a wry smile and said, 'But we've rather strayed from the reason I'm here this morning, haven't we?'

'Y-yes,' she stammered, tinglingly aware that her hand still rested in his. 'I'm sorry, I shouldn't pry into your private life . . .'

'Don't apologise, Kate it warms my heart to know there are sincere and kind people around such as yourself. But, as I'm sure you will appreciate, I can't discuss my problems with my patients, they would lose confidence in me yet, at times, I am just as vulnerable as they are.'

She nodded; her eyes fastened on his as if in a trance. And when he rose to go she pulled herself together to ask, 'What shall we do about the key?'

'Don't worry, I'll see you get a new lock fixed tomorrow. Meanwhile, make sure you push the bolt home as well.'

There was no call from Godfrey. And by the next morning Kate was becoming extremely annoyed over his neglect of her career, rather than heartbroken as a result of his silence.

But now she had to consider her future, a future in which she had begun to suspect Godfrey did not wish to be a part of. Alex had said she shouldn't waste her time on him, advice she now was sure her father had prompted. But, her father's opinion aside, before she could start to make alternative plans she wanted to hear what Godfrey had to say.

She was surprised by the speed at which Godfrey lifted the receiver, but when she heard, 'I'll be with you in a moment, darling,' and sensed the suggestive note in his voice when he continued, 'unless you would like to join me here?' she felt anger rising.

'Godfrey! You haven't replied to my call,' she reminded him icily.

'Oh dear, it's you, Katie! Sorry old thing, more people to see, but don't worry I'll ring you back . . .'

'Oh no you won't Godfrey. I want to know this very minute if you have arranged an audition for me?'

'Sweetheart, you are so impatient, what's the hurry?'

'Well, if you have to know I must make plans to travel to London . . .'

'You mean here, to my place?'

'No, I don't think so, not your place,' she said bitterly. 'It sounds to me as though I've already been replaced!'

'Aw, Katie, cool it, darling, I'll ring you, I promise . . .'

'You and your promises!' she retaliated. 'You promised to arrange for me to play with a top concert orchestra, said it was all in hand for the new season . . .'

'Darling, I will, trust me,' he cajoled. 'In any case, we've got to impress your father. Don't want to upset him, do we?'

'We, or you? I doubt my father will be influenced by anything you do.'

'No, Katie, you're wrong. I'm intending to persuade him to back the company. We need more facilities—bigger offices in a more up-market area, you know . . . something of advantage to us both so don't let me down.'

'Too late, Godfrey, I'll find another agent. Obviously, I can't rely on you.'

His tone changed. 'Don't forget I'm your agent, we have a contract.'

'An empty threat,' she returned as calmly as she could. 'And, as I have not signed any contract I am quite free to decide my own future . . .'

'Well, don't expect to have a career with a top orchestra!' he retaliated. 'For one thing, you don't have an ounce of talent, and for another you haven't got the glamour, or the figure, and that's what it takes . . .'

It took Kate a while to simmer down after the exchange with Godfrey Downes, though she had managed a casual farewell before she switched off her mobile. Obviously, his ego had taken a blow, though she was determined not to allow him to think she had been hurt by his cutting remarks.

Now she decided the best cure for her tangled emotions was work, and she set about cooking breakfast for Martha and herself. And she was relieved to see the television was turned on when she took the tray upstairs. With any luck, her conversation with Godfrey would not have been overheard.

She had just started on her dish of creamy porridge when her mobile began to ring. Suspecting it was Godfrey, furious over her rejection of him, she didn't immediately reply, but when the ringing was persistent she switched the mobile on and remained silent.

'Kate? Katherine?' she heard Alex Blair query, and the mere sound of his voice sent her spirits soaring and she snatched up the phone.

'Yes, Alex, I'm here . . .'

'Can you be free for an hour or two later this morning?'

'Not really,' she declined slowly. 'I don't like to leave Martha . . .'

'No problems there,' he said. 'Nurse Garbutt was planning to call on her this morning—perhaps get her downstairs—so I thought it an ideal opportunity to take you down to Elmsgarth with me.'

'Oh yes, I'd like that. Has the condition of the road improved?'

'Well, shall we say I won't be calling for you on horseback,' he said with laughter in his voice. 'We should be fine in the Land Rover.'

'Thanks, I shall enjoy a change of scenery.'

'I could pick you up about a quarter to

eleven.'

Doing a little twirl of pleasure, she skipped back to the table to finish her breakfast in haste. No time to waste, if she was to be ready by a quarter to eleven she had better get on with the chores.

Martha's initial response when she told her of the promised outing was merely a smug little smile. 'I knew you would grow to like him,' she said as Kate was leaving the bedroom. 'Off you go, my girl, get yourself ready. A change will do you good, and you might get me a quarter of peppermints while you're there.'

Kate's heart sang as she changed into a soft woollen suit in a shade of blue that she knew suited her well. But she hesitated over her footwear, realising the high black boots were her only suitable choice. They didn't look too bad after the soaking they got on her first few days here, it was amazing what a good polish could do. With her hair brushed and shining, and wearing a hint of make-up, she went to Martha's room to seek her approval before going down to wait.

'We'd never wear such short skirts in my time,' the older woman remarked. 'But at least you've got decent legs so I suppose it's not too bad.'

Kate twirled in front of the long mirror and said, 'It's down to my knees.'

'I think I hear that mobile thing ringing,'

Martha interrupted, her head to one side. 'Did you leave it downstairs?'

'Yes, it's in the kitchen,' she said, 'I hope my outing isn't going to be cancelled—I suppose it can be difficult for doctors to make plans.'

Kate's cheerful 'Hello' when she switched on the phone was quickly dampened when she heard Godfrey's voice.

'Katie, darling,' he began, 'I'm ringing to apologise, I shouldn't have spoken to you that way this morning . . .'

'True, you shouldn't,' she responded calmly.

'Oh. So can I take it I'm forgiven?'

'No, you can't,' she replied firmly.

'Believe me, Katie, you can depend on me, and if you can put in a good word for me when you next speak to your father we can really go places.'

'You are quite free to go to any place you wish, Godfrey Downes, but I won't be going with you so don't call me again,' she ended coldly and switched off.

There, she had managed to sever her connection with the Downes Company but, much to her distress, she began to sob almost uncontrollably and hot tears streamed down her cheeks.

Fumbling in her bag for a handkerchief she dabbed her eyes and tried to control the gasping sobs that shook her slim body. And when she heard a knock on the door she strove to compose herself and glanced at the clock to see it was just half past ten.

Opening the door to the nurse and Alex, she avoided looking directly at him as she murmured a greeting and indicated for them to enter.

'Are you still in your bed, Martha?' the nurse called from the foot of the stairs. 'You can prepare to come down for a couple of hours while there's enough muscle to give you a hand.'

Kate heard Martha's exclamation of pleasure, and without turning in Alex's direction said, 'She'll be delighted to come down.'

She was unaware of his look of concern but he didn't ask any questions and merely explained, 'We're earlier than I expected, but I thought it would give us an opportunity to spend a little more time in Elmsgarth.'

Swallowing hard, she nodded and said a little shakily, 'I'll go and help Nurse Garbutt and make them coffee before I go . . .'

'No, no, I'll do that,' he said, reaching out a restraining hand.

It wasn't long before he and Nurse Garbutt appeared with a smiling Martha walking slowly between them. 'There,' Alex said as he lowered her into a chair, 'you'll feel better for a spell down here. We shouldn't be much more than a couple of hours, but I intend to call on the old couple who live at the Manor—see how they are today,' he said, with a meaningful glance at the nurse.

Giving Martha a swift kiss on her cheek, Kate kept her face averted as she followed him to the vehicle outside.

'The conditions aren't quite so bad this morning, so I managed to do most of my round in this,' he told her as he slid into the driving seat and switched on the powerful engine. 'I've just left young Peter, he's doing remarkably well. He'll be going to hospital for a check, of course.'

He drew the vehicle to a halt and she sensed his eyes upon her before his fingers slid beneath her chin to bring her round to face him.

'What is it?' he asked softly as she struggled to avoid his eyes.

'It's nothing, really,' she gulped.

'Oh, Kate, I don't like to see you like this,' he said, cupping her cheek in his warm hand. And he drew her towards him, resting her head against his shoulder to murmur soothing words until her sobbing ceased.

'I'm sorry,' she said on a shuddering breath and took the folded handkerchief he offered. 'I don't know why I'm like this.'

He looked down into her tear-filled blue eyes and smiled. 'No need to talk until you're ready, we have plenty of time.'

Alex's comforting words helped her regain a little of her composure and she began to feel the need to explain her distress. Looking up at him she moved slightly away, preparing to speak, but he drew her back, his hand on her cheek when his lips met hers in a brief but gentle kiss.

'Perhaps you will find it easier to talk as we drive along,' he suggested.

'Thanks, I appreciate that,' she began and went on to relate the conversation she'd had with Godfrey that morning.

He listened and nodded, allowing her to pour out her troubles until she began to recover from her distress. 'Obviously, I can't depend on music for a living after what he said,' she said bitterly. 'If he hadn't encouraged me for all this time I could have trained for something else.' Her lower lip trembled.

He reached over and gave her hand an affectionate squeeze. 'No, Kate. Every experience is valuable, a means of preparing for the future.'

She shot him a tremulous smile, and with a slight quaver in her voice she confessed, 'I hadn't thought of it like that.'

'I found it helped me when I was your age.'

She looked at him with fresh interest. 'I wouldn't have thought you felt like that, not when you were training to be a doctor.'

Alex chuckled and told her, 'At sixteen, all I wanted to be was a professional footballer and play for Scotland. I spent every spare moment chasing a ball around until someone told me

I'd never make it, I wasn't fast enough.'

'And are you glad you didn't? I mean, what a waste of your medical skills.'

'Glad? Believe me, I wouldn't change my present occupation with any footballer, not even a star player.' He uttered a contented sigh and added, 'Yes, I remember I was furious at the time, but soon realised I owed a lot to the sports teacher who criticised my speed.'

She nodded. 'But it is a bit late now for me to change my career. Actually, my aim was to teach—I wanted to give piano lessons to children.'

'And why did you not follow your original plan?'

'Because I was very naïve. Godfrey Downes scoffed at the idea, persuaded me to let him act as my agent, promised he'd get me work with a top orchestra.' She gave a soft sigh and continued, 'Soon after that, unfortunately, I injured my wrist and it has taken quite some time to fully recover—almost a year in fact.'

'I see. Well, you shouldn't take notice of what Downes says,' he advised. 'Believe me, Kate, you are a very attractive and extremely desirable woman, and still young enough to pursue a career.'

'Thanks,' she murmured dropping her eyes. 'Maybe I am young enough, but playing the piano is all I know. Except for a temporary job in the local hospital when I first left school, music is all I've ever studied.'

'Ah yes, the hospital—was the hospital work a good experience?'

'Yes, I suppose it was really,' she murmured thoughtfully.

'Then it was a valuable experience in your life. I observed your warm and caring nature during our emergency with young Peter the other night.' He smiled, drawing the vehicle to a halt by a wide gateway when he reached over to pat her hand. 'Certainly not the ice maiden I first thought you to be.'

She laughed. 'Thanks for the compliment, Alex, but I hadn't realised I gave that impression. Ice maiden indeed!'

'There,' he said, 'now you're laughing again. Feel better?'

She nodded. 'Yes, thank you for listening, I feel much better now.'

'Then you won't mind if I call at the Manor. There are a couple of elderly people I'm rather concerned about.'

'Oh yes, Peter said something about a robbery there.'

'I expect he heard me mention it to his mother—it shook them up terribly.'

Kate watched him turn to walk up the tree-lined drive, her heart a little lighter now. Looking out at the wintry scene around her she experienced an ache of pleasure, seeing the beauty of nature in the sparkle of thawing icicles, and hearing the slither of snow as it fell from the laden tree branches.

Now she hadn't the ties of her career to worry about she felt a surge of happiness over the freedom on offer.

CHAPTER SIX

Alex was soon back in the driving seat, satisfied his patients were both safe and well. 'I was relieved to learn their daughter is staying with them for a couple of weeks. By then we might have this problem solved.'

'What problem, Alex? Was it more than just a robbery—were they injured?'

'No, no, they are fine,' he said and concentrated on making his notes which to Kate appeared to be his way of closing the subject.

Although Elmsgarth was sheltered from strong north-east winds racing over the moor, Kate found it still bitterly cold when she alighted from the vehicle. Their first call was to purchase a lock for the door of Hawthorn Cottage when Alex had the assistant cut extra copies of the key.

'This time we won't hang one in the shed,' he said. 'Providing you agree, I think it best if the nurse and I have one and you keep one for your own use.'

'Of course, I must rely on you for advice.' She looked up at him and queried, 'But is the decision to have a new lock and no spare key in the shed in any way connected with the robbery at the Manor?'

'Better be safe than sorry,' he quoted lightly. 'Now, where shall we go next?'

'Did you not want to go to your surgery, Alex?'

'Yes, but there's no need for you to go. It's not far, just round that corner,' he told her, raising his hand in the direction of the church. And glancing at his watch he suggested, 'If you like, Kate, you can continue with your shopping, and I'll meet you back here in half-an-hour.'

Kate watched him stride away in the direction of his surgery, wondering why he avoided giving a direct answer to her questions.

Remembering her time was limited she set off across the market square, calling at the confectioners for the peppermints Martha requested, plus a couple of magazines and a colouring book for Peter. Next, she went to the grocery store to buy ingredients for a pasta dish that would add variety to their weekly menu, and included a bottle of red wine.

She did consider purchasing some small token of gratitude for Alex but couldn't decide on what to buy. Perhaps instead she would invite him to dinner with the excuse of it being a meal to celebrate Martha's return to better health.

Hearing the chime of the church clock, she realised it was time to return to the place she and Alex had arranged to meet. As there was no sign of him she continued to stroll in the direction he had taken, expecting to meet him on his way back, but when she turned the corner she spotted him, his back towards her, speaking to a policeman.

As Alex was not aware of her being there, she paused a short distance away. But as she waited by the church wall, his voice carried over to her clearly when she heard him say to the officer, 'I realise it must be a problem for you to keep watch on them all, particularly in these conditions. All I'm able to do is try to persuade a relative to stay with them until this business is cleared up.'

'That's a good idea, Doctor, and you can rest assured the sergeant is doing his utmost to bring in more men . . .' she heard the policeman respond. Then his voice faded as he turned away from Alex to speak to someone passing by.

Not wishing Alex to think she was eavesdropping, Kate retraced her steps back to the corner. Only minutes later Alex came up beside her but made no mention of his conversation with the policeman. She hadn't the courage to question him about what she had overheard, but felt sure it was connected with the robbery at the Manor.

'Is it too cold for you?' he asked, noting her

frowning expression.

'No, I'm fine,' she said as they strolled back across the market square. 'I'm just wondering if there's anything I've forgotten.'

He smiled at her. 'I usually ring the grocer with my order. You could do the same, then let me know and I'll pick it up when I'm down at the surgery.'

'That's kind of you, but as soon as the road is clear I'll get out my own car.'

'Still planning to return to London?' he asked, his voice casual but his eyes intent on her face as he waited for her response.

She sighed. 'I'm not sure, there's no urgency in making a decision. Fortunately, I've got a little money in reserve which gives me time to make plans.'

'I'm really pleased to hear you will be with Martha a while longer. She's certainly benefited from having your company.'

'My only regret is not having a piano here,' she told him and giggled as she added, 'I should have played a flute—the ideal portable instrument!'

'That can be easily solved, Kate. You can come over to play the piano at Ivy Lodge whenever you wish.'

Her expression brightened. 'Oh, I'd love to, if there is someone with Martha, that is. Do you play?'

'No, but my father used to enjoy playing, and young David Bowman often came to listen. Actually, David became quite keen and used to practice a little piece my father taught him so I've always kept the piano regularly tuned.'

'Oh, Alex, that's great!' she exclaimed delightedly.

'I shall enjoy hearing you play. It seems always so depressingly quiet now my father's gone,' he remarked.

Seeing sadness in his eyes she said, 'And I shall enjoy bringing music back to Ivy Lodge. In fact, I'm very glad I won't have to rush back to London after all.'

'That's what I wanted to hear,' he said, smiling down on her. 'And perhaps you will have dinner with me as well?'

'Yes, Alex, I'd like that very much.'

'Once Nurse Garbutt is not required to stay with Peter so many hours each day, I'll ask her to spend an evening with Martha,' he proposed eagerly. 'They seem to get along together very well.'

'Mmm, they never stop chattering.' She laughed, then her expression became more serious when she asked, 'How is Peter now?'

'Yes, he's doing very well, in fact, once the lock has been changed you'll be able to go and see him for yourself.'

'True, I won't be so anxious. Not that I intend going out for any length of time,' she quickly assured him. 'Just a short visit to the Bowman's place.'

'Ask David about his piano playing whilst you are there. If he's still keen, why not give him a lesson?' he suggested.

She looked up eagerly. 'Oh could I? I didn't like to presume, but the thought had crossed my mind.'

'Right, that's settled. Now we had better finish our shopping, and if time allows we can go over to the White Swan Hotel for coffee.'

Kate's spirits had lifted considerably, and she was content to wait until Alex paid for his box of provisions that would be delivered to his Land Rover parked near the White Swan. With sufficient time for refreshment they moved on to the hotel, Alex finding her a seat in the lounge before excusing himself to go and have a word with the receptionist. Returning to his seat as coffee was served, she saw his eyes narrow, seeming to observe everyone who came in or passed by outside.

'Are you expecting someone?' she asked, noting a slight tension in his manner.

He shot her a quick simile. 'No, no, I'm sorry, I was merely interested to see who comes in here these days.'

'Well, I must say, it's a comfortable place,' she said, looking around her. 'Is it an hotel the locals use?'

'No, doubt it. I should think visitors to the area make up the clientele. We must come here for dinner one evening once everything is settled.'

'That would be nice,' Kate murmured, but she wondered what it was that must be settled, and why suddenly had Alex become so tense?

On the journey back to Hawthorn Alex appeared rather preoccupied, and twice she had to repeat something. 'Did you say John is coming to fix the lock this afternoon,' she asked as he drew his vehicle to a halt outside the cottage.

'Er—yes, I'll remind him,' he said, coming round to help her out.

'I must pay you for the lock,' she said, gathering together her handbag and shopping.

'Don't worry about that just now, I'm a little short of time,' he told her, and picking up her shopping he followed her to the cottage door.

'Oh I see, well I won't forget. And thank you so much for taking me to Elmsgarth this morning, and listening to my problems.'

He shot her a brief smile. 'My pleasure,' he said then, as he turned to go, added, 'Unless Nurse Garbutt prefers to walk, John will give her a lift home.'

'Why didn't you invite the doctor in?' Martha asked as Kate put down her bags.

'He was in a hurry to get away otherwise I would have done.'

Nurse Garbutt glanced up sharply to ask, 'Has he been called out?'

'Not to my knowledge, unless there was a message for him at the surgery.'

The nurse shook her head. 'No, there are no

calls at the surgery now, all calls are transferred to the doctor on duty.'

'Isn't there a receptionist at the surgery?' Kate queried.

'Not nowadays, oh no,' the nurse informed her with a mirthless smile. 'The doctors' take surgery, of course, and the district nurse has a clinic. So, patients either telephone, or leave a note as we don't want any more problems there.'

Kate frowned. 'What problems? I do wish someone would enlighten me.'

'Doctor Blair doesn't like us to talk about it so better not.' Nurse Garbutt gave a knowing nod.

Kate had to stifle her curiosity, as it was obvious the nurse was unlikely to disclose anything further. But she was convinced it was something connected with the doctor's receptionist.

It was two hours later when John arrived to fix the new lock. 'The doctor asked me to check your car whilst I'm here,' he said. 'We think the battery will be flat.'

'Yes, I'm sure you're right. I've not turned the engine over since I arrived.'

'If it's the battery I'll get it charged for you, no problem,' John offered.

John had the lock changed in a very short time, and pocketing a key for Doctor Blair, he pressed another into her hand, reminding her to keep it in a safe place. 'And here's one for the nurse,' he said, handing her a second, 'though now you're staying on here it may not be necessary.'

Staying on? For one moment the words surprised her, yet there was something rather comforting about knowing she didn't have to face London and Godfrey. To use Alex's piano to keep up her practice made the idea even more tempting.

She suddenly became aware that John was speaking. 'I'm sorry,' she said. 'What was it you were saying?'

'I was wondering how soon you need your car. Doctor Blair tells me you want to visit the Bowman's, and maybe you'll want to go down to Elmsgarth again.'

'Yes, that's right, I'd like to see how Peter is getting on,' she said, a little disheartened to hear that Alex had not included her visit to his home.

Once John and the nurse had left, Kate took up a tray of tea and cakes bought that morning.

'Oh, these do look good!' exclaimed Martha. 'What a lovely change.'

'Yes, I enjoyed doing a bit of shopping today,' Kate agreed. 'Considering Elmsgarth is only a small town it has a surprising number of shops.'

'I'm pleased you went, and I knew you would find the Doctor good company,' Martha said, and went on to enquire, 'By the way, did you call at the Manor?'

'Yes, but I waited in the Land Rover whilst Alex made his visit.'

'Oh, so it is Alex now, is it?' Martha said with an impish smile. 'I wondered how long it would take you two to become friendly. Now, tell me, how are the old folk at the Manor? I've been quite worried about them, theirs is the fourth robbery in this area in the past few weeks.'

'Fourth! Martha, how do you know that? You've been in hospital . . .'

'Ah yes, but I heard about them when the Vicar made his weekly hospital visit. I didn't say anything but I've noticed all four robberies involved elderly folk and all are Doctor Alex's patients.'

Kate's eyes widened. 'Oh, that's dreadful! I hope no violence was involved.'

'Only the first one—a retired chap—owner of the local stables, he was tied up and gagged. You see, he put up a fight which is why he came off worst.'

'But the police, haven't they been able to catch those responsible?'

Martha shook her head. 'I don't know what things are coming to.'

'Now don't you worry, you're perfectly safe here,' Kate assured her gently.

'Then why did John come to change the lock on my door?' Martha returned shrewdly.

For a moment Kate was stuck for words.

She also had wondered why the simple solution of cutting another key had been ignored. 'I'm not sure, maybe the weather had affected it,' she offered, though she was becoming increasingly aware something was not quite right.

'Weather, pah! It had been no bother up to now,' insisted Martha, screwing up her mouth. 'When I see that doctor of ours I shall ask him if everyone over sixty in his practice is having their locks changed!'

'Now don't upset yourself. No-one's going to break in whilst I'm here.'

'But I can't expect you to stay on here, you have your own life to lead.'

'Believe me, I wouldn't leave if anything's troubling you,' Kate promised. 'Anyway, I've had an offer you'll want to hear about. Shall I pour another cup?'

Kate took a long breath and began to relate all that had happened regarding Godfrey, finishing with Alex's suggestion for her to use his piano. 'You see, I can't keep up my practice here so I was thrilled when he invited me to his home.'

Martha nodded. 'Yes, that had occurred to me. Pity there's no piano here, but it's thoughtful of the doctor to offer you the use of his. Ivy Lodge is just off the road to Elmsgarth, not too far away.'

Kate was delighted over the prospect of going to Alex's home to play the piano, but as there was no further word from him she was beginning to wonder if he had regretted his offer. And she had been disappointed when there was no sign of her car the following day but felt it impolite to telephone to ask why. However, the following afternoon John drove up in her car and asked if she would mind running him back to the Doctor's house.

'Now you have a new lock, leaving Miss Cussons shouldn't be a problem,' John said.

'And now I have the car back I can make a quick visit to the Bowman's tomorrow. I haven't seen Peter for a couple of days.'

'I believe young Peter is going to hospital tomorrow . . .'

Kate glanced up anxiously. 'You don't mean there's something wrong?'

'No, he's fine,' John assured her. 'The doctor just wanted to have him checked to be sure everything is all right.'

She smiled. 'I'll never forget that night . . .'

'I know, you were terrific . . .' he began, but Kate shook her head.

'Oh no, I did very little. All the credit goes to you and Al—er, Doctor Blair.'

John shot her a smiling glance. 'Better tell Miss Cussons we're going,' he suggested. 'The road is fairly clear of ice now so it shouldn't take long.'

Driving to within two miles of Elmsgarth, John pointed out a turning on the main road and directed her along a tree-lined drive towards the large house ahead.

'Here we are, Ivy Lodge,' he announced as he got out the car. 'The Doctor is down at the police station just now.'

'Sounds ominous,' she remarked. 'Do you expect trouble?'

'No, the other doctor will deal with any call-outs.'

'I wasn't thinking of call-outs,' she said. 'Miss Cussons mentioned there's been four robberies and all involved Doctor Blair's patients. Surely, that is more than coincidence?'

John nodded. 'Yes, it looks that way, but the doctor has the matter in hand now so the problem will soon be resolved.'

'Well, I'd better not keep you,' she said when it became obvious John was not likely to divulge anything further.

Going carefully up the hill on her way back to Hawthorn Cottage, Kate felt her spirits sink. Had Alex been at home she'd planned to invite him to Hawthorn for a meal and maybe then she would have discovered what this mystery connected with the robberies was all about.

During lunchtime the next day, Kate's mobile rang and she was delighted to hear Alex's voice. 'May I call on you this evening, Kate?'

'Yes, of course,' she replied, striving to keep the excitement from her voice.

'It could be rather late as I must stay until surgery is over.'

'Would you like to have a meal with me, Alex?'

'Well, if it is no trouble,' he said, and without waiting for her assurance continued. 'What time can I expect you?'

'Around half past eight, I guess, if that is not too late for you?'

Kate seemed to have difficulty finding her voice. 'That's fine,' she quavered happily. 'I'll look forward to seeing you.'

Kate's mind was in a whirl when he'd gone from the line. What was it he wanted to talk about, she wondered and, equally important, what was she to wear? And should she risk cooking something new?

When Kate mentioned this arrangement to Martha she saw her faded blue eyes light up. 'Perhaps I can have my supper a little earlier than usual,' she suggested, 'make it a bit easier for you.'

'Are you sure you wouldn't like to come down again? You managed very well with only my help today.'

'No I would not, thank you all the same. I've already had a good lunch and I can't eat heavy meals late at night. Besides, my favourite programme is on at half past seven.' Martha smiled as she went on to advise, 'You just forget about me and concentrate on cooking him a nice meal. He'll appreciate that.'

CHAPTER SEVEN

Kate found it difficult to quell the excitement rising within her as the evening drew near. She had prepared the ingredients for her planned Italian dish and laid places at the small table in the alcove at one end of the kitchen considering it much cosier than the rarely used dining-room.

Remembering to open the wine, she polished the glasses she'd discovered in a cupboard left over from when her father was here.

The fire burned brightly, its warm glow reflected in the gleaming copper jugs and horse brasses hanging from the beams. The place looked inviting, and she realised with certain surprise that this was somewhere she could happily make a home for herself. And with a bit of rearranging of furniture there may be room for a piano . . .

Once Martha's supper had been served, Kate changed into a cream woollen dress, noting with increasing impatience there was still half a hour to wait until Alex was due to arrive. When finally she heard a vehicle draw to a halt outside her heart increased its beat and she had the door already open before he reached the house and heard the vehicle drive away.

'I took a taxi,' he explained. 'My car let me down in Elmsgarth otherwise I would have been here ten minutes ago. I hope I haven't kept you waiting?'

'No, perfect timing,' she said as he stepped into the warm kitchen. 'The meal should be ready now, unless you prefer to relax first.'

'Mmm, something smells good, makes me feel relaxed already.'

'Good, then I'll serve,' she said, pulling on her oven gloves. 'If you would care for a glass of wine you can pour for us both.'

'Certainly, I shall enjoy this. John will pick me up when I'm ready so I'm not driving tonight. I brought a bottle of wine with me so we won't run short.'

'What exactly had you in mind when you asked if you could call tonight?' she queried, placing the bubbling dish on a mat in the centre of the table. 'I mean, was there something important you wanted to say?'

'Nothing that won't keep until we've enjoyed this,' he said, smiling.

'I hope you enjoy it,' she murmured, taking a sip from her glass, 'and then, after you have told me what this visit is about there is a question I'd like to ask.'

The meal was a success and Kate was delighted. 'Would you like dessert,' she suggested, 'or shall we finish the wine?'

He studied her for a moment then nodded as he refilled their glasses. 'Yes, it'll give us a chance to talk and by the expression on your face it appears to be serious business you wish to discuss.'

'I believe it is,' she said, resting her elbows on the table as she leaned towards him. 'You see, I sense there is something going on in this place, some sort of mystery, and I'm anxious about it.'

'Then tell me, Kate, exactly what is it that worries you?' he asked as he continued to hold her gaze across the table.

'There are a number of things, actually,' she began, taking a steadying breath. 'For instance, why did you need to get a new lock for this place, why not just have another key cut? Even Martha couldn't understand that.'

'Simply a safety precaution,' he said. 'If anyone has found the other key they will be unable to use it.'

'Like the man who called here—the one you questioned me about?'

'Well, there was no point in alarming you,' he said gently. 'In any case, the police have the matter in hand.'

'And I assume you felt it necessary to find a companion for Martha so, between you, you and my father organised my visit here. Am I right?'

He smiled and raised his hands in a gesture of resignation. 'Yes, you're right, Kate, and let no-one suggest you are naïve—far from it! But believe me when I tell you Martha's well-being wasn't the only reason your father asked you to come here. He also was most concerned about your association with Godfrey Downes after certain details of his rather dubious reputation came to light. Downes was using you as a means to stay on favourable terms with your father.'

Kate bowed her head. 'Yes, and I'm beginning to suspect he had persuaded my father to part with his money once before,' she admitted flatly. 'I have no feelings for Godfrey Downes whatsoever now.'

He reached for her hand. 'I'm so pleased to hear it,' he said. 'And if you'll allow me to pull your chair round to this side of the table we'll drink to that.'

Now, seated next to Alex, she felt his hand slide across her shoulder, drawing her closer as he raised his glass to say, 'To a lasting friendship,' and clinked it against hers.

'To a frank and honest friendship,' she replied. 'And to clarify another matter, tell me what became of the receptionist who used to be with the practice?'

He groaned and turned his head away. 'Please don't bring that up, Kate, it has no connection with us.'

'But it is somehow connected with other problems here—I'm sure of it!'

'Who has been filling your head with these ridiculous stories?'

'Alex, don't stall,' she said, moving away

from him. 'You did have a receptionist, now you don't, but as no-one will discuss it that means there is something suspicious about her leaving. I know it is none of my business but I'm concerned about you.'

His dark brows drew together. 'I see,' he murmured and reached over to draw her back. 'I've had a few problems, yes, but I didn't realise you cared so much.'

'Of course I care, that's only natural I would have thought.'

'But is your concern for me only natural, as you put it, or dare I hope for something more?'

Confused, Kate dropped her eyes, twirling the stem of her glass as she replied, 'I'm not sure how I feel, but I don't like to see anyone under stress.'

He tilted her face with a finger, compelling her to look into his eyes. 'I'm sorry, Kate, I can't say anything just yet, and I want you to promise me you won't discuss it with anyone. As I told you, the matter is in the hands of the police.'

With one dark brow raised, he continued to hold her gaze, closing the space between them until his warm lips captured hers in a lingering kiss.

'Oh, Kate,' he groaned, turning in his chair so that he could enfold her in his arms. 'I have wanted to do this from the moment we first met.'

'And you did, if you remember?' she whispered. 'I had only been here a day or so and I must admit you took me by surprise . . .'

'Ah, yes, but I have known of you for much longer. What you don't realise is, I've known you forever. My father had photos of you and your parents from years ago, when you used to visit here all the time.'

She laughed. 'But you didn't recognise me when I first arrived.'

'Because it was dark and you weren't expected until the weekend. However, when you told me you were heading for Hawthorn Cottage, this gout-ridden old fool soon realised your father had managed to persuade you to leave earlier.'

'Oh dear, I do apologise,' she said, her hand on his cheeks. 'It wasn't meant unkindly . . .' she went on as her fingers came into contact with the scar beneath his jaw making him jerk back his head.

'I'm sorry, Alex, is it painful?'

'No, not any more,' he said picking up his glass.

'How did it happen—did you fall off Prince or . . .'

'Something else I'd rather we didn't discuss until I am at liberty to tell you the full story.'

She shrugged. 'As you wish, I don't want to add to your problems.'

Looking directly into her eyes, he said, 'Trust me, Kate, please. I need both your trust and your friendship more than you realise.'

'All right I will, and I promise not to ask too many questions.'

'Ask what you like, providing it is not connected with my profession.'

'But you're not in any danger, are you?'

He grinned. 'No, nothing so dramatic.'

'In any case, I'd never divulge anything you had told me.'

He rose to his feet and drew her up to join him. 'My dear, sweet little ally, I need you so much,' he murmured, 'but now I must ring for my transport and leave you.'

'Must you, Alex . . .?' she began only to be silenced by his eager lips in a kiss that left her almost breathless.

After John drove Alex away, it took Kate a while to compose herself sufficiently to attend to Martha's needs before she went to her own room.

It had been a perfect evening and, thankfully, the Italian pasta dish had been a success. But it had been quite a shock for her to discover in only a little over a week she had become so attracted to Alex Blair, a man who confessed he had felt close to her for years.

The phone call Kate received the following morning convinced her that she hadn't been dreaming when Alex invited her to his home to play the piano.

'Nurse Garbutt happened to mention she was calling on Martha so I asked if she would mind making it this afternoon,' he said. 'I hope that suits you?'

'Oh yes, thank you, I'd love to play. What time is suitable?'

'And I would love to hear you,' he said warmly. 'Nurse should be with you around three-thirty so come as soon as you can. I can't offer you a meal equal to the one you cooked last night, but I'll try to rustle up something tasty . . .'

'Please, Alex, don't worry about food, the opportunity to play is enough.'

'For me it is an opportunity to be with you,' he murmured.

Kate's heart sang as she rushed through the morning's chores. She had already prepared the vegetables for lunch when she had a sudden urge to make cakes—one to take for Alex, and another to leave for Martha and the nurse's tea. And straight after lunch she planned to visit Peter Bowman.

Thankfully, the battery had held its charge and the engine of her little car sprang immediately to life. Kate was delighted to find young Peter was recovering well. She wanted to ask Mrs Bowman if she knew what had become of the receptionist at the surgery but not wishing to break her promise to Alex she suppressed the desire. But she was curious and for some unaccountable reason felt certain there must be a connection between what had happened at Alex's surgery and the robberies on his elderly patients.

Back at the cottage she was about to make sandwiches to leave for Martha and the nurse, when her father rang. Delighted to hear his voice she told him the news. 'Martha is making good progress. In fact, she will be coming down any minute now. I'm usually with her of course, but she is able to get up and down the stairs without too much help.'

'Good. Incidentally, Kate, has the house telephone been connected yet?'

'No. I did ring the company and the engineers will be out again tomorrow. They tell me the wires had been cut.'

'Well, at least you have the mobile, but remember to keep it charged.'

'I will. Incidentally, I'm going over to Alex's place to play the piano. It was kind of him to offer—'

'Have you something planned?' he broke in sharply.

'No, I just need to play—exercise my fingers—no other reason than that,' she said and heard him utter a small sigh before she added, 'By the way, you will be pleased to know I have severed my connections with the Downes Company.'

'Kate, darling, you have no idea how relieved I am to hear that. I didn't feel inclined to back that unscrupulous devil a second time after I heard about his womanising last year.'

'I am glad you haven't, and I'm only too

sorry I didn't listen to you before. I have been terribly gullible. I really regret my stupidity and hope you weren't too much out of pocket because of it.'

'Frankly, the money doesn't matter. In any case, the last time he approached me he didn't get anywhere near the amount he asked for, and since I discovered what his little game is, this time I firmly refused.'

She gave a short laugh. 'I hadn't realised Godfrey could be so devious, but I think being up here has brought me down to earth.'

'Then stay as long as you like, Kate. I know Martha won't mind.'

'But life here is not as tranquil as I first imagined, you know. There have been a few robberies in the area, and Alex has had the lock changed which makes me suspicious though he's determined not to give me a reason. In fact, he asked me not to discuss it with anyone . . .'

'Then best not, but don't worry, Alex will ensure you are in no danger, he knows what he's doing.'

'And by that I guess you also know what he's doing,' she surmised with a chuckle, 'so I suppose I shall have to contain my curiosity.'

'Just be patient, darling,' he advised, 'enjoy playing the piano at Alex's place. Oh yes, I'll have a word with the telephone people before I leave, make sure you are reconnected. I have some business to complete in Rome so if you don't hear from me for a few days you'll know the reason.'

Once the nurse had arrived, Kate felt able to leave and with the carefully wrapped cake in one hand and a bag containing her lighter shoes in the other she went out to her car. After a day of mainly sunny weather the light had not yet begun to fade and she negotiated her way between the gateposts on to the road with ease.

A short distance from the cottage she saw a dark blue four-wheel drive vehicle parked in a gateway on her right and noticed both the driver and passenger quickly avert their heads as she drove slowly past on the narrow road. It had appeared to be a man in the driving seat, and a woman seated beside him draping a scarf over her head. Normally, she would have taken scant notice but it was a glimpse of the woman's flaming red hair that caught her attention.

Kate frowned. Not many cars parked in this area, particularly as the high ground beside the road afforded only a restricted view of the surroundings. Perhaps they were tourists.

Arriving at Ivy Lodge ten minutes later, she was surprised to see Alex standing in the open doorway. 'Just checking to see if you had found your way and not gone past the turning.'

'No, John showed me where you live. I brought him back here after he delivered my car. I believe you were away at the time.'

Alex nodded. 'Ah yes, he mentioned it. I assume Nurse Garbutt has arrived?'

'Mmm, everything's fine,' she told him as they went indoors. 'I paid a quick visit to young Peter after lunch. He's been to hospital for a check up, I hear.'

'Yes, it was a great relief when I received the call to inform me all was well. It can be a bit risky you know.' Taking her coat he hung it in the panelled hall and offered his arm as support whilst she changed into her shoes. Nodding towards the parcel on the table he queried, 'What have you got there?'

'Cake,' she said simply, 'freshly made today. I hope you like it.'

He looked down on her and smiled. 'A pretty face and a good cook, heh? Quite a catch for any man.'

Any man? She felt a sudden stab of dismay. Did he appear as if she was trying to inveigle herself into his favour? The way to a man's heart and all that . . . She shrugged, her cheeks growing warm.

'So Martha has got round to cake-making already, has she?' he said, his lips quirking with amusement. 'She's certainly making progress.'

Flustered, Kate turned away from his smiling face. 'Where do you have your piano?' she asked. 'I've been looking forward to this.'

'In here,' he said ushering her across the hall in to a large comfortably furnished lounge with a grand piano standing beside French windows.

'Oh, the light will be perfect,' she smiled and hurried over to the beautifully polished instrument. 'I don't have any music with me, of course, but I think I can manage a few pieces without.'

He chuckled and shook his head. 'It never ceases to amaze me how musicians can memorise quite long pieces without having a sheet of music in front of them.'

'Practice,' she declared. 'After playing it many times it seems to stick in the memory, and there is a pattern to the work of many composers when certain phrases are repeated.'

To ease her nervousness, Kate ran her fingers up and down the keyboard, playing scales before she introduced a gentle Debussy number. Then, as her confidence grew, she changed key to play the stronger chords of a Chopin Polonaise.

It was not very long before Kate was lost in the pleasure of making music when time passed unnoticed. But when she tried out a less rehearsed piece and struck a wrong note, she paused and became suddenly aware of Alex standing nearby.

'Sorry, Kate, I didn't mean to interrupt, just needed to get another folder.'

'It's all right, it wasn't your fault, I need the music for that one,' she admitted. Then, glancing at her watch exclaimed, 'Goodness, is it that time already!'

'Please, just play the Debussy one more time. I find it so relaxing and you play it extremely well.'

'Oh, thank you. It's also one of my favourites, and this is a beautiful instrument on which to play it,' she said, smiling as she caressed the highly polished wood at the end of the keyboard.

Having no response she assumed he'd gone back to his work, but hearing a soft sigh she glanced up to find him still beside her, a serious expression on his face. 'I hope it hasn't prevented you working?' she said, starting to rise.

But immediately she felt his hand on her shoulder when he said, 'No, certainly not, and I hope you will soon come here again.'

'I'd love to, if Nurse Garbutt is around, that is . . .'

'But there are times when you will need to go out,' he broke in to say, 'and Martha does have an emergency call button to hang round her neck.'

'Oh does she? I hadn't realised. I must ask her where it is. When we have the telephone reconnected she should feel more secure when I'm out.'

'Most likely it's been put away in a drawer,' he suggested. 'Many of my older patients seem reluctant to use what they refer to as new-fangled things.'

She laughed. 'That is exactly what Martha called my mobile.'

He nodded. 'Why don't you continue playing whilst I rustle up a tray of tea?'

'I think that's enough for this time,' she said as she straightened her shoulders and flexed her fingers, 'but I would appreciate the opportunity another day—if it doesn't interfere with anything you are doing, of course.'

'Come whenever you wish,' he invited as he went to stand behind her, gently massaging the muscles of her shoulders with his strong, capable hands. 'In fact, I can let you have a key in case John is out.'

She held her breath, sensually aware of his touch, and there was a tremor in her voice as she struggled to reply. Then, as though regretting the action, he quickly lifted his hands away, suggesting they go through to the kitchen to take tea.

'We could make sandwiches,' he suggested, opening the door of the refrigerator, 'but I don't seem to have much to offer until the provisions arrive.'

She shook her head. 'Thanks, but I'm not very hungry just now.'

'Then why don't I take you out to dinner this evening?'

'Oh, but I should get back . . .'

'Martha has your mobile, hasn't she?'

Kate laughed. 'Yes, she carries it with her

from room to room.'

'Good, then we can go down to Elmsgarth for an early meal. And before we leave I'll ask Nurse to get out the panic button and remind her how to use it ready for when your line is connected.'

'You think she'll be all right on her own?'

'If I know Nurse Garbutt, she won't be in a hurry to leave. She and Martha have plenty in common—they're of an age—so let's have a cup of tea and a slice of the cake you brought.' He looked at his watch to add, 'If we leave soon there will be time for you to look round the shops whilst I call in at the surgery in case there are any messages or letters for me.'

CHAPTER EIGHT

Leaving her little car at Ivy Lodge, she rode with Alex down to Elmsgarth where he parked his vehicle in the market square. She found a number of shops still open, their window lights inviting on this cold, dark evening.

'I really like these attractive little shops,' she said as she got out, 'but I won't delay you. Shall I meet you back here at six?'

'No hurry. You do your shopping then come over to the White Swan. If you are first there order a drink, though I don't expect to be too long.'

'Can I get anything for you?' she asked as he started to walk away.

He turned and smiled, his eyes twinkling in the light of a street lamp. 'Only your sweet self,' he said softly before he continued on his way.

Smiling to herself, Kate wandered off towards the newsagents. But passing the window of a small shop selling ladies' fashions she spotted a matching set of trousers and sweater in a warm shade of red. Not having prepared for a long stay at Hawthorn she was pleased to find something suitable for the climate.

By the time she had tried on the outfit and paid the assistant, she saw the lights in most of the shops were being turned off and she just had time to call at the newsagents to purchase a few magazines and mints for Martha.

'Lucky to have caught me,' the gentleman behind the counter said in his strong Yorkshire accent, 'I was about to shut up shop.'

'Lucky indeed,' she replied. 'I know Miss Cussons wouldn't like to have missed some of her favourite mints.'

'So you're staying with the lady at Hawthorn, a relation I expect,' he said with a knowing nod. 'How is she keeping these days?'

'Oh, quite well really, thank you. Improving all the time.'

'Not had any trouble with these crooks we keep hearing about, has she?' he wanted to know. 'There's been three or four burglaries already, so tell her to keep the place well fastened up.'

'I'll make sure she does, never fear,' Kate assured him and gave a small shudder as thoughts of the burglaries returned.

Going across the Square, she entered the White Swan Hotel. At first there was no sign of Alex, then she spotted him through the glass door where he appeared to be in earnest conversation with the receptionist. Crossing the empty lounge to take a comfortable chair by the open fire, she pondered over what they could be speaking about and experienced an unexpected stab of jealousy. But she had no right to think of Alex as exclusively hers she reminded herself and ordered a glass of wine to quell the sudden emotion.

Gazing unseeingly at one of the magazines she'd purchased, Kate wasn't aware that Alex had come into the lounge until he said, 'Why so serious?'

'No reason,' she replied as casually as she could manage.

'I see you managed to catch the shops,' he remarked, noting the fashion label on the larger of the bags. 'Anything nice?'

'Mmm, a lovely red trouser suit, and at a very reasonable price.'

'And friendly service?'

She laughed. 'Yes, very different from London. The newsagent assumed I was a relative of Martha's and advised me to tell her to keep her doors locked because of the robberies round here. And goodness knows what else he'd have had to say if he hadn't been about to shut the shop.'

'Ah, but what you may not realise is that it is also a safeguard. Everyone knows who lives around here, more or less. The receptionist here has been of great help to me. Call it nosiness if you like, but at least they all look out for each other and if someone has a serious problem then they warn everyone else . . .'

'But he mentioned three or four robberies that have happened locally,' she broke in to point out, 'so how is it the robbers keep returning to this area?'

'Not for much longer,' he said with a thoughtful nod. Then, as though he had only just become aware of what their conversation was about, his expression quickly changed. 'Let's see what is on tonight,' he said and went over to the bar to fetch a menu.

Thinking it wiser to match his change of mood she said, 'Can I get you a drink?'

'Mmm, just a tonic water for me, I'm driving.'

'Next time I'll drive then you can relax.'

He gave her a lingering look and reached for her hand to say softly, 'I'm very pleased to hear there will be a next time, Kate. Very pleased.'

'Well, it appears as though I shall be here at least until my father is back in this country as I don't fancy the idea of being in London without him,' she admitted.

'Ah yes, that was something I wanted to speak with you about and as we're on our own here it gives us a good opportunity to talk.' He picked up his glass and leant back in his seat before he went on to say, 'Do you recall telling me you would like to give piano lessons?'

'Yes, but that was before my other plans were thwarted. I've got the necessary qualifications, of course, but, like I said, it would mean going back to London.'

'Why London?' he asked. 'Why not here in Elmsgarth? The last music teacher has only recently retired and it has left a lot of young musicians without hope of continuing their musical careers.'

'Oh, that is sad,' she murmured, 'they must be dreadfully disappointed. But you surely aren't suggesting . . . ?'

'Why not? The teacher's health has failed considerably in the last few months—such a shame as her pupils were doing extremely well.'

She looked at him, her eyes wide. 'And you think I could fit in here?'

'I can't think of a reason why you shouldn't. As a matter of fact, Kate, I was going to arrange for David Bowman to have lessons, and the lad was really keen to start, but when the lady became ill we had to cancel our plan.'

'Poor David. If he was as keen as you say then it must have been very disappointing for him . . .'

'Which brings me to the point of this conversation,' he said, looking directly in to her eyes. 'Would you be interested in teaching David? He could have his lessons at Ivy Lodge and, naturally, I would be more than willing to pay.'

Her brows lifted in surprise. 'Are you serious, Alex?'

'Of course. It would be an introduction to a new career for you, and if you found it satisfactory we could install you and a piano somewhere in Elmsgarth.'

'But I wouldn't expect you to pay me . . .'

'Oh yes, Kate, I already intended to pay for David, it was all arranged.'

'But, Alex, why are you doing all this for me?'

He felt for her hand and held her gaze as he broke in softly, 'Because, my dear Kate, I very much want you to stay.'

Her heart fluttered as she looked into his eyes and said, 'You do . . . ?'

'I most certainly do,' he agreed, and drawing her to her feet suggested, 'We ought to go and eat now or the Bistro will get very busy.'

The intensity of Alex's gaze when he voiced his desire for her to stay left Kate a trifle stunned. She was aware he liked her but this sudden admission of his feelings had been so unexpected. He continued to be most attentive throughout the meal, and when the time came to leave he linked his arm through hers to escort her to his Land Rover, which was parked across the Square. And once they were back at Ivy Lodge he helped her transfer her purchases to her little car before taking her in his arms to give her a lingering farewell kiss.

'Promise you'll ring me as soon as you get back, Kate,' he reminded her as they drew apart. 'I want to be sure you are safely home. And give some thought to the piano lessons, won't you? I know David would be delighted if you stay,' he continued, adding softly, 'and so would I . . .'

There was a warm glow somewhere in the region of Kate's heart as she got into her car and started the engine, grating the gears in her haste to acknowledge his wave before reversing to drive away in the direction of the main road.

* * *

It started to rain heavily during the journey back to Hawthorn Cottage and Kate switched on the wipers, reducing her speed as she hummed along with a popular song on the radio. She was simply bursting to tell someone, share the delight she'd felt when Alex repeated his desire for her to stay.

After all, it was what she had studied for, and music gave her the most pleasure in her life—well, not quite she mused, wallowing in the memory of Alex's kiss.

The downpour had begun to subside by the time she reached the wood a short distance from the cottage. But the visibility had not improved and even though most of the snow had melted the surrounding fields seemed dark with little to see of the countryside beyond the headlights. As she drew up at the cottage gate she thought she glimpsed a reflection from another vehicle parked near the hedge further up the road, then dismissed it as probably the reflectors of a tractor parked up ready for the morning.

Alighting from the car, she crossed over to the wide gate leading into the garden and glanced up to see a glow of light in Martha's bedroom window as she swung the gate open. It appeared Nurse Garbutt had made sure Martha was safely up the stairs before she left Kate realised gratefully, remembering her promise to phone Alex as soon as she got indoors.

Returning to the car, Kate drove carefully through the gateway and parked beneath the apple trees at the rear of the house. Taking her parcels she got out and locked the car, pausing a moment when she thought she heard an unfamiliar sound. Once she had adjusted to the darkness she felt in her pocket for the key, but as she raised her eyes on her approach to the door her heart lurched. She realised she was not alone.

The shock of seeing two dark figures standing by the door rendered her momentarily speechless and the key fell from her fingers, but she managed to summon enough courage to demand, 'Who are you, what do you want?'

'The key, if you please,' a male voice responded softly, his hand outstretched.

'Certainly not! This is a private house,' she told him sharply.

'Now, hand over the key . . .' he hissed.

'I will not!' she cried stepping away from him. 'You have no business here. I shall call the police!'

'If the lock hadn't been changed it would have saved you a lot of trouble,' he snarled. 'As it is, if you can't be reasonable I shall have to resort to force.'

Protesting furiously Kate tried to push him aside, but his companion sprang forward to grab her wrist, yanking her almost off balance. By the painful stab of sharp fingernails, Kate quickly realised it was a woman she was grappling with, and when she felt the man take her other arm in an excruciating grip she let out an ear-piercing scream.

'Shut her up!' the man commanded. 'I'll get the key . . .'

Kate felt the man search her pockets and let

out another high-pitched cry. But the woman quickly pressed a hand over her mouth and pulled back her head, stifling her efforts to continue. Not that anyone would hear her, she knew, but she wasn't going to give in without a struggle and she sank her teeth into the fleshy part of her assailant's finger.

The woman yelped snatching her hand away. 'Jack, she bit me! Do something, can't you!'

As the man closed in Kate kicked out at him, but this time the woman pulled her totally off balance bringing her crashing to the ground. She then felt her handbag being yanked from her shoulder and saw the man empty its contents on to the step, flicking his lighter to help find the key amongst them.

And it was in this small flickering light that Kate saw the woman a little more clearly and realised it was the person she had seen in the parked car beside the road earlier, the woman with the startling red hair.

Determined not to give in, Kate struggled to her feet and before the woman could grab her again she spread her hands and gasped, 'Please, just tell me what you want? There's nothing in the house of any value.'

'Shut it!' the man snarled and flung down her handbag in disgust. Then, gripping her jaw in his bony fingers, he hissed, 'The key, where is it?'

'It's not in the usual place,' the woman put

in, 'I've had another look.'

'So,' he began, tightening his hold, 'you've found a new hiding place for it.'

Kate knew this man meant business and racked her brain for a solution to her predicament as she struggled to escape his painful grip. But she felt a tiny surge of satisfaction when she knew he hadn't spotted it falling from her hand.

The key would be lying in the muddy ground somewhere beside the garden path.

'Go and have another look in the shed!' he instructed the woman. And digging his fingers into Kate's jaw he threatened, 'If you want to make it easier for yourself you'd better speak up or I might have to leave my mark on that pretty little neck of yours as well!'

As well? Could he be referring to the scar under Alex's chin? Desperate to escape, Kate yanked back her head, catching a glimpse of movement in an upstairs window when she shrieked, 'Let me go—I'll tell the police!' hoping Martha would hear. But until the telephone was connected, the emergency call button was useless. Would Martha think to call for help on the mobile?

'Oh yes, and do you think the plod from Elmsgarth will hear you!' he sneered, pinning her arms by her sides. 'And the old woman in there can do nothing about it—we cut the wires before you got here last week.'

Kate shook her head and decided it may be

wise to play for time. 'Look, why can't we discuss this,' she began, and offered, 'You can have my purse, my watch, anything you like but just let me go.'

'The key?' he prompted as the woman came back to report no key was to be seen. 'Come on, where is it?'

'I had it in my coat pocket.' Kate lied. 'It must have fallen out when I got out of the car . . .'

Nodding towards the redhead he instructed, 'Search the car. You'll find the car keys on the step.'

With her arms still pinned she tried to remain calm whilst the woman searched the car, eventually coming back to say, 'It's not there, Jack, but I found a torch.'

'Well use it, stupid!' he grated. 'Search the garden between the car and the house . . .' Suddenly, his voice tailed off and Kate felt his hold tighten at the sound of an engine when powerful lights swung on to them as a police car came through the open gateway, closely followed by a Land Rover.

In the beam of light Kate saw two uniformed men running towards them, but they came to a sudden halt when the man quickly slid one arm round her neck.

She heard a metallic click and froze when she caught the gleam of a blade only inches from her face.

'Release the girl!' one officer commanded

as the other continued to advance towards them.

'Come any closer and she gets this!' the man hissed, brandishing the knife in front of her eyes.

'Don't be stupid, man, you'll only make it worse for yourself,' the officer warned, taking a step forward. 'Come on, hand over the weapon.'

'No way,' the man snarled, tightening his hold round her neck. And to the woman with red hair he demanded, 'Get the car—bring it here—quickly!'

Terrified though Kate was, the dim figure of Alex in the background gave her courage and she strove to think of a means of escape. She noticed the officer who had remained silent had retreated into the shadow of the police car, but then she spotted him skirting the hedge towards the shed. And as Alex started to advance towards them from the other side the red-haired woman held back.

'I'm telling you, Blair, she'll get this,' the man warned, raising the hand holding the knife towards Alex. And to the woman he demanded, 'Now go on, what are you waiting for? He won't dare to touch you while I've got this one.'

The woman hesitated. 'Oh, Jack, are you sure . . . ?'

'Get moving!' the man cried angrily.

'Perhaps she's not as stupid as you thought,'

Alex jeered provokingly. 'She knows you'll not get away with it this time so why not give yourself up now . . .'

'If you don't mind, Doctor, we'll handle this,' the first officer advised. And it was then Kate realised her captor's attention was on Alex and the officer, and from the corner of her eye she caught a glimpse of the other policeman closing in behind.

Quickly raising one foot, she scraped the heel of her shoe sharply down on the man's shin with as much force as she could muster.

He yelped and hollered and made to increase his hold on her, but this was when everything seemed to happen at once. The officer came swiftly from behind, disarming the man in one rapid movement, pushing Kate away to safety whilst the other officer cornered the woman. And before she could collect her wits Kate found herself caught in Alex's firm grip.

'Can we leave the lady in your hands, Doctor?' the policeman asked as the handcuffed villains were being led away. 'We'll get statements from you later.'

'Yes, leave her with me,' Alex replied. But as the police car drove off Kate felt her legs would give way beneath her and she sobbed with relief as Alex enfolded her in his arms.

'Kate, you're shaking, let me get you inside,' he said softly.

'We can't, I dropped the key,' she explained

unevenly, 'it's somewhere on the path . . .'

'Don't worry, darling, I have mine here,' he said, releasing her to reach into his pocket for the duplicate.

Once the door was open he helped her in to the warm kitchen. 'Just sit quietly for a moment,' he advised, and examining her bruised neck he queried with concern, 'Does your neck hurt very much?'

'No, I'll be fine,' she said bravely, fingering her neck with care. 'But tell me, am I right in thinking that woman was your receptionist?'

'Yes, she was,' he agreed, stressing the last word. 'I had strongly suspected her of searching through my patients notes, making copies of them, and I've since discovered the man with her is her brother.'

'And was he the cause of that scar under your chin?'

Alex sighed. 'Yes he was, though I didn't see his face at the time. You see, one night I returned to Ivy Lodge to discover a hooded man looking through the files on my computer. When I challenged him he attacked me with a knife before escaping. I didn't have a clear view of him but tonight I recognised his voice.'

'That must have been awful for you,' she said in a tremulous voice. 'I can't imagine what he would have done to me if you hadn't arrived.'

Very soon Martha entered the room, her

face lined with concern. 'She'll be fine,' Alex assured her. 'It wasn't a pleasant experience but she was very brave.'

'But why did they come here,' Kate asked. 'Were they after money and valuables—is that what they expected to find?'

'Yes, I realised the notes they were interested in were only those of both elderly and wealthy patients,' he explained, 'so I decided to contact the police.'

She clutched his arm. 'Oh, Alex, I don't know what would have happened to me if you and the police hadn't arrived when you did.'

'And you also have Martha to thank,' he told her, sending the older woman a smile. 'She alerted me on your mobile and I contacted the police.'

'Ah no, it was easy,' Martha said, brushing his praise aside. 'But I think I'll go back to my bed now and leave you to look after Kate.'

'It will be a pleasure. Goodnight, Martha.' Turning back to Kate he said, 'I suggest we have a cup of tea, then I'll leave you something to ensure you get a sound night's sleep.'

She managed a smile as she said, 'Yes, Doctor, anything you say.'

He gazed fondly down on Kate and reached for her hand. 'Yes, that was your Doctor speaking, and if you take my advice you will allow him to kiss you after you have promised to let him look after you for the rest of your life. You see, he loves you very much and hopes you won't go away.'

'Yes, Alex,' she murmured happily. 'I have already decided I want to stay.'

'As my wife, Kate?'

Kate merely smiled and pulled his head down until their lips met.